A HOLIDAY NOVELLA OF THE UNNATURAL BRETHREN

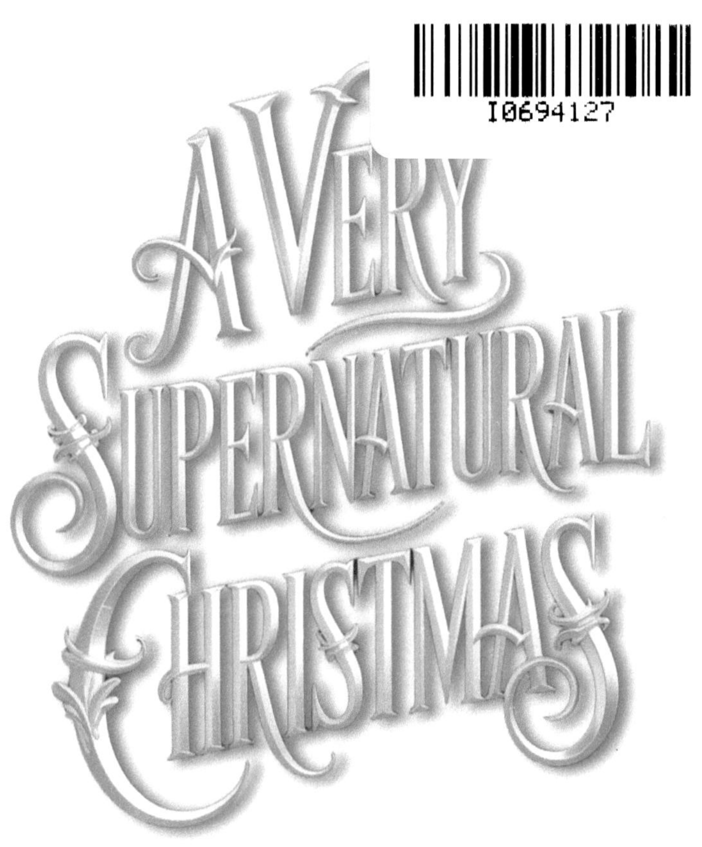

USA TODAY BESTSELLING AUTHOR

SILVANA G. SÁNCHEZ

BOOKS BY SILVANA G. SÁNCHEZ

THE UNNATURAL BRETHREN

Written in Blood

Call of Blood

Cast in Blood

Blood and Mistletoe

Blood and Bargains

A very Supernatural Christmas

Midnight Kiss

BAD BOY SHIFTERS OF THE
UNNATURAL BRETHREN

Branded in Love

Runt of the Pack

Embers of Fate

Branded in Memory

Wings of Shadow

CURSED KINGDOMS

Ash and Snow

Steel and Stone

Cinders and Blood*

Vesely Academy

Academy of Extraordinary
Creatures

The Soul Thief

Curse the Moon

The Blood of Kings

Be the first to know when Silvana's next book is available! Follow her on Bookbub to get an alert whenever she has a new release, preorder, or discount!

*For everyone who ever felt like
they didn't belong at the family
table—
until they built their own.*

Someone I loved once gave me a box full of darkness.

It took me years to understand that this too, was a gift.

— MARY OLIVER.

MY FREE AUDIOBOOKS

Do you like FREE audiobooks?
Go check out my YouTube channel!
Subscribe and get notified when new books are up!

A NOTE FROM THE AUTHOR

My Dearest Darklings,

Christmas comes but once a year.

Unless you're a pregnant witch with unprecedented magical power and a flair for the dramatically absurd—in which case, Christmas comes whenever you damn well please.

Welcome to December, my beloved readers. Welcome to the season of impossible hope wrapped in winter darkness. Welcome to a celebration that has no business existing and yet demanded to be written.

You see, I couldn't let this year end without giving you—my faithful darklings, my Darkling Coven, my partners in gothic romance—one more chance to spend time with the characters who've claimed our hearts (and occasionally tried to rip them out).

This novella is my gift to you.

Not because you deserve sweetness and light

(though you do). Not because the holidays demand happy endings (though we'll see about that). But because you've walked with me through blood-soaked ballrooms and resurrection spells, through branding ceremonies and dragon curses, through every dark moment where love bloomed anyway.

A word about timing: This story takes place months after the events of *Blood and Bargains,* serving as a bridge to the upcoming *Blood of the Ancient.* Pay close attention, darklings—there are hints woven throughout about what's coming. Threads are being pulled. Secrets are surfacing. And the darkness that's been building? It's about to break.

You've earned this chaos.

You've earned Ivan's sarcasm and Cassandra's optimism. Gavriil's penance and Dristan's devotion. Dragons fighting over thrones while a toddler makes it snow indoors because feelings are complicated and magic doesn't care about your dinner party.

So pour yourself something suitably dark and satisfying (hot chocolate, strong coffee, mulled wine, or straight bourbon—I support all choices), settle into your favorite reading spot, and join me for one *very* supernatural Christmas.

The fire's burning. The snow's falling. The family's gathering.

And nothing—absolutely nothing—is going to go according to plan.

Exactly as you like it.

With wicked love and dark devotion,
  Silvana

P.S. Yes, there's mistletoe. Yes, it's weaponized. No, I'm not sorry.

CONTENT WARNING

*A **Very Supernatural Christmas*** contains mature themes and content that may not be suitable for all readers. Please review the following content warnings before reading:

Explicit sexual content - Strong language - Violence and magical combat - Pregnancy - References to past trauma (non-consensual magical bonding) - Death and grief - Dark magic and curses - Family conflict and emotional tension

Recommended for readers 18+
Reader Discretion Advised.
Note: This is a work of fiction featuring supernatural beings. The behaviors depicted should not be emulated in real-life relationships.

Please read with care.

A VERY SUPERNATURAL CHRISTMAS

They survived blood magic and resurrection spells. Can they survive Christmas dinner?

Six months pregnant and wielding unprecedented power, witch Cassandra Deveraux has decided that her dysfunctional supernatural family needs something impossible: a Christmas celebration. In May. Because timing, like family, is what you make it.

The guest list reads like a supernatural disaster checklist:

- One cynical vampire who's allergic to optimism
- Two rival dragon shifters fighting for the same throne
- A bear king willing to atone for unforgivable sins
- A wolf-witch toddler whose emotions control the weather

- And enough ancient grudges to fill a Gothic novel

What could possibly go wrong?

Everything.

But beneath the chaos lies something real: the truth that family isn't about perfect moments. It's about broken people choosing each other anyway. About showing up even when you'd rather burn the place down. About finding light in the darkest places.

Pour the mulled wine. Light the candles. And pray the guests survive the night.

A Very Supernatural Christmas is a gothic holiday tale of found family, second chances, and the beautiful disaster that happens when vampires, shifters, and witches gather under one roof.

A Very
Supernatural
Christmas

IVAN LOCKHART

Ho ho ho and welcome to hell, darkling.

Picture this:

A vampire. A Christmas tree. And a pregnant witch whose magic keeps setting said tree on fire.

Now add two dragon shifters who want to kill each other, a bear king everyone else wants dead, a child whose emotions control the weather, and enough centuries-old trauma to fill a Gothic novel.

That's the party I'm walking into tonight.

Welcome, dear darkling, to what might be the most catastrophically ill-advised holiday celebration in supernatural history.

For those of you who don't know me—and in that case, shame on you—I'm Ivan Lockhart. Three hundred years old, devastatingly charming, and deeply skeptical of anything that requires optimism or emotional vulnerability. You might know me as the vampire who's mastered the art of sarcasm, survived the French Revolution, and recently watched his ex-lover return from the dead by stealing her descendant's body.

Yes, that actually happened.

No, I'm not going to explain it twice.

The point is, I recognize a disaster when I see one.

And tonight's Christmas party? *Disaster* doesn't even begin to cover it.

Let me set the scene for you, since you're clearly coming along for this ride—because, let's face it, this isn't our first rodeo.

The Location: Deveraux Manor. Ancient. Magical. Currently decorated with enough Christmas lights to be visible from space, despite it being May 17.

The Host: Cassandra Deveraux. Witch. Six months pregnant with a vampire's child. Has set her Christmas tree on fire three times already, and we haven't even started the party. Believes in things like "family" and "holiday spirit" with the kind of earnest optimism that should have died out in the Middle Ages.

The Guest List: Oh, where do I even begin?

My maker, Dristan, who turned me into a vampire three centuries ago without asking permission. We have what psychiatrists would call "unresolved issues."

Juliette—the woman I loved in 1672, who died, and who recently came back by commandeering her descendant's body. We're... working through it.

Gavriil Alexeev, the bear shifter king, who branded Cassandra five months ago in a forced magical bond.

Dristan wants to murder him. I'm considering offering assistance.

Two dragon shifters fighting for the same throne who are absolutely, definitely not going to cause a supernatural incident tonight. Absolutely not.

A toddler wolf-witch whose magic responds to emotions. Because nothing says "festive gathering" like weather controlled by an infant's feelings.

This is starting to sound less like a guest list and more like "The Twelve Days of Christmas." *Two rival dragons, a bear king in a pear tree, and a partridge that controls the weather...*

You see the problem.

This isn't going to be one of those heartwarming holiday stories where everyone learns valuable lessons about love and togetherness while snow falls gently outside and someone plays piano.

This is going to be chaos.

Glorious, ridiculous, possibly violent chaos.

And I'm going anyway.

Why?

Excellent question. One I've been asking myself for the past week.

The answer, unfortunately, involves admitting that somewhere beneath my carefully cultivated cynicism, there's a part of me that actually wants this to work. That hopes Cassandra's impossible optimism isn't entirely misplaced. That wonders if maybe this collection of damaged supernatural creatures can actually be something resembling a family.

That part of me is clearly an idiot.

But he's a hopeful idiot.

So here's what you need to know before we begin, dear darkling:

Christmas is a human holiday. It celebrates the birth of a god who would absolutely condemn creatures like me. Vampires don't *do* Christmas. We don't *do* nativity scenes or advent calendars or any of the performative nonsense designed to make mortals feel better about their inevitable deaths.

We certainly don't *do* Christmas parties in May.

But Cassandra asked.

And somehow, that mattered enough to get us all here.

So welcome to *A Very Supernatural Christmas.*

There will be fire—literal and metaphorical.

There will be arguments. Old wounds reopened. At least one supernatural confrontation, possibly two.

There will definitely be no snow, unless the child cries.

But maybe—just maybe—there will also be something real. Something worth the absolute chaos we're about to witness.

Or it'll be a complete disaster, and I'll spend eternity saying "I told you so."

Either way, you're coming with me.

The tree is already on fire.

Let's see how much worse it can get.

Follow me into the night, darkling. I promise you'll have a blast.

Possibly a literal one, if those dragons start fighting.

IVAN: THE ANNOUNCEMENT

"It's a Christmas tree," I say flatly, staring at the massive evergreen currently levitating through the front doors of Deveraux Manor. "In May."

"Mm-hmm," Cassandra hums, guiding the tree with effortless waves of her magic, violet flames dancing at her fingertips. The damn thing must be twelve feet tall, perfectly shaped, and completely inappropriate for the current season.

I pinch the bridge of my nose. Three hundred years of immortality, and this—this—is going to be my undoing. Not hunters. Not ancient vampire courts. Not even Juliette's death and miraculous return from the seventeenth century.

No. I will be defeated by a pregnant witch throwing Christmas. In spring.

"Cassandra," I try again, employing the patient tone

usually reserved for explaining modern technology to Dristan. "Christmas is in December."

"Your observational skills remain sharp, Ivan." She sets the tree down with a gentle *thud* in the great hall's center, right where the Louis XIV settee used to be. Used to be, because it's now shoved unceremoniously against the wall, buried under boxes labeled "ORNA-MENTS" and "LIGHTS" in Cassandra's aggressive scrawl.

The tree stands there, accusatory in its evergreen glory, shedding needles onto Juliette's priceless Persian rug.

"Christmas," I say slowly, as if speaking to a particularly dim fledgling, "is in *December*. December twenty-fifth, to be precise. It has been December twenty-fifth for approximately seventeen centuries. The date is rather firmly established."

Cassandra turns to face me, hands on her hips—well, where her hips used to be visible before the pregnancy. She's wearing an oversized black sweater that says "WITCH PLEASE" in silver letters, leggings, and fuzzy socks with tiny snowflakes on them. Her dark hair is piled on top of her head in a messy bun, held in place by what appears to be a candy cane-striped pencil.

She looks absolutely ridiculous.

She also looks happy. Genuinely, radiantly happy in a way I haven't seen since before... well. Before everything went to hell last winter.

"Christmas," she says, violet flames flickering in her

storm-grey eyes, "is whenever I say it is. I'm the one who almost died breaking a magical brand with resurrection magic."

"That's not how—"

"I'm *also* the one carrying unprecedented magical power while very pregnant." She takes a step toward me, and I swear the air temperature drops several degrees. Or maybe that's just my survival instincts kicking in. "Do you *really* want to argue with me right now?"

I open my mouth. Close it. Look at the Christmas tree. Look at Cassandra's determined expression, at the way her magic crackles around her like a living thing, at the slight swell of her belly where an impossibly powerful child grows.

Look at the seventeen boxes of decorations.

Look at the garland already hanging from the chandelier.

Look at my chances of winning this argument.

Sigh.

"Where do you want the ornaments?"

She beams, and damn it all, her smile is infectious. "I *knew* you'd come around."

"I'm not coming around," I mutter, moving toward the nearest box with the reluctance of a man approaching his own execution. "I'm capitulating under duress. There's a difference."

"Semantics." She's already levitating another box, this one labeled "LIGHTS – GOTHIC" because, of course, she has a specific aesthetic vision for this madness. "Besides, you love me."

"I *tolerate* you. Barely."

"You love me," she repeats, sing-song, as she begins wrapping the tree in what appears to be black and silver fairy lights. Because even Christmas in May must be appropriately gothic.

I pull an ornament from the box—a delicate glass skull with a tiny Santa hat painted on it. Of course.

"When is this catastrophe happening?" I ask, examining the skull. It's actually quite well-made. Trust Cassandra to find macabre Christmas decorations.

"Saturday."

I nearly drop the ornament. "This Saturday? As in, three days from now?"

"Mm-hmm." She's not even looking at me, too focused on making the lights perfectly asymmetrical in that specific way that looks accidentally elegant.

"Cassandra." I set the skull down very carefully. "Please tell me you're not planning what I think you're planning."

"If you think I'm planning a full Christmas Eve dinner with all of our friends and family, complete with Secret Santa gift exchange, gothic feast, and enough holiday cheer to choke a reindeer—" She finally looks at me, grinning like a madwoman. "Then yes. That's exactly what I'm planning."

"No."

"Yes."

"Absolutely not."

"Absolutely yes."

"You're insane."

"I'm *festive*." She descends from her levitating position—showing off, really—and crosses to me. Her hand finds mine, and I feel the warmth of her magic, the steady pulse of life in her veins. "Ivan. I need this."

The playfulness drops from her voice, and I see it then. The shadow beneath the smile. The memory of last Christmas, when Gavriil had branded her against her will, when Dristan had been forced to leave because of the spell, when she'd been alone and terrified and trapped.

When she'd spent Christmas in this manor, powerless and pregnant, not knowing if any of us would survive to see spring.

But we did survive. We're all here. Alive. Together.

And she wants to celebrate that.

Even if the timing is completely absurd.

"Fine," I hear myself say, and I'm not even sure when I decided to surrender. "But I'm not wearing a Santa hat."

"We'll see about that." She's already pulling another box toward us, this one making ominous jingling sounds. "Now, help me with the stockings. We need thirteen."

"Thirteen?"

"Thirteen." She starts counting on her fingers. "You, me, Dristan, Juliette, Gavriil, Luciana, Samara, Nikolaas, Clarissa, Kaisner, Vlad, Anya, and little Katya."

I stare at her. "You invited Gavriil."

"I invited everyone."

"The man who branded you against your will."

"The man who gave Dristan back to me—with his grief for Luciana," she corrects quietly. "And the man who's trying. He's trying, Ivan. That has to count for something."

I want to argue. Want to point out that "trying" doesn't erase trauma, doesn't undo what was done. But I see the set of her jaw, the determination in her eyes, and I know this argument is already lost.

Besides. She's right. Gavriil is trying. And if Cassandra can extend an olive branch wrapped in Christmas lights and questionable timing, who am I to object?

"You're going to give me stress-induced grey hair," I mutter.

"You're a vampire. You can't get grey hair."

"Oh, you'll find a way."

She laughs, bright and clear, and begins hanging stockings on the mantle with magic. Each one is black velvet with silver embroidery—names in elegant script. Mine is already hung, right next to Dristan's.

"Wait," I say, processing the guest list. "Vlad is in town? I thought he was in Russia with Anya and their daughter."

"Business trip," Cassandra explains, hanging Vlad's stocking. "He mentioned it last week. Said he'd be in Paris through the weekend. So obviously, I invited him. And then Anya surprised him by flying in with Katya, so now they're all coming."

"Of course they are." I shake my head. "Vlad hasn't spent a proper holiday with the family in years. He's going to have no idea how to handle this chaos."

"That's what makes it fun." She grins wickedly. "Besides, little Katya is the most magical thing I've ever seen. If anyone can make Christmas in May feel legitimate, it's a wolf-witch toddler who makes it snow indoors."

She has a point. I've heard the stories.

"This is going to be a disaster," I say, but I'm already reaching for another box of ornaments.

"Probably," she agrees cheerfully. "But it'll be *our* disaster. Our family. Our completely absurd Christmas in May."

She's not wrong.

God help us all.

I hang the skull ornament on the tree, right at eye level, where everyone will see it, and I can't help but smile.

"You're already mentally planning your outfit, aren't you?" Cassandra asks, reading me too easily.

"I will neither confirm nor deny."

"Dark green velvet? With the silver collar chains?"

"I said nothing."

"And probably the antique pocket watch."

"You're insufferable."

But we're both smiling now, and as I help her decorate this ridiculous out-of-season Christmas tree in Juliette's formal parlor, I realize something:

Cassandra is giving us all a gift. Not presents

wrapped in paper and ribbons—though knowing her, those are coming too. But the gift of joy. Of celebration. Of choosing to embrace life and family and absurdity in the face of everything we've survived.

She's choosing to make new memories to replace the painful ones.

And if that means Christmas in May, complete with gothic decorations and vampire attendance and probable disaster?

Well.

I've certainly participated in stranger rituals over the centuries.

"The invitation says 'festive attire encouraged,'" Cassandra adds, pulling out what appears to be a garland made entirely of black roses and silver bells.

"Please tell me you're not expecting us to wear ugly Christmas sweaters."

Her grin turns positively wicked.

"Cassandra. No."

"I'm just saying, there's a very nice one with a vampire Santa that would look—"

"Absolutely not."

"—amazing on you with those cheekbones—"

"I will burn it."

"—and Dristan already agreed to wear his."

I freeze. "Dristan agreed to wear an ugly Christmas sweater?"

"Well." She hangs the garland on the mantle, artfully arranged. "I may have used my *feminine wiles*."

"You're diabolical."

"I'm in love." She pats her belly. "And hormonal. It's a devastating combination."

I can't argue with that.

"Three days," I say, more to myself than to her. "We have three days to prepare for the most chaotic dinner party in supernatural history."

"A *very* supernatural Christmas, yes," she confirms. "Better get shopping. Oh! Speaking of which—" She disappears into the hallway and returns moments later with a small crimson velvet bag, the kind that might hold jewelry or perhaps, knowing Cassandra, cursed artifacts.

"No," I say immediately.

"You don't even know what it is yet."

"I know that tone. That's your 'Ivan is going to hate this but do it anyway' tone."

"Secret Santa!" She shakes the bag with entirely too much enthusiasm. The contents rustle ominously. "Everyone has to draw a name. It's tradition."

"It's not tradition if you invented it three days ago."

"I invented it three *weeks* ago, actually. I had everyone draw names when I sent out invitations. Everyone except you, because you kept avoiding me."

She thrusts the bag toward me.

I stare at it as if it might contain a live snake. "Can't I just buy a generic gift for the group?"

"That defeats the entire purpose of Secret Santa."

"The entire purpose seems to be creating social anxiety and awkward gift exchanges."

"Exactly!" She shakes the bag again. "Come on, Ivan.

Don't make me use pregnancy hormones and witch magic to compel you."

"You wouldn't."

"Try me."

We lock eyes. I've known Cassandra for years. I've seen her face down ancient vampires, resurrect an Ursa King's lover from beyond death, and survive magical brands that should have killed her.

She absolutely would.

With a long-suffering sigh worthy of a three-century-old vampire, I reach into the bag. My fingers brush past a carefully folded paper. I grab it—the last one—and pull it out.

"Once you draw, there's no going back," she warns.

"What am I, five years old?"

"You're acting like it."

I unfold the paper.

Stare at the elegant script written in what appears to be calligraphy ink.

Gavriil Alexeev

My blood runs cold. Well. Colder than usual.

"So?" Cassandra leans forward, trying to peek. "Who'd you get?"

I carefully refold the paper and slip it into my jacket pocket, my face carefully neutral. "That's rather the point of *Secret* Santa, isn't it?"

"Oh, come on—"

"I'm following the rules." I head for the door with as

much dignity as I can muster. "Now, if you'll excuse me, I need to go shopping."

"Ivan, wait—" But she's laughing now, one hand pressed to her belly. "You got someone difficult, didn't you? Your face went all tight and British."

"My face is *always* British. I'm English."

"You know what I mean!"

"Fine. Yes. I drew someone complicated." I turn back, and she's watching me with that knowing expression that means she's already figured it out. "But I'll handle it."

"You'll handle it," she repeats, clearly skeptical.

"I'm three hundred years old, Cassandra. I think I can manage Secret Santa."

"Can you?"

Before I can answer, Dristan appears in the doorway from the parlor, holding what seems to be a tangled mass of Christmas lights. How he managed to knot them when they were stored perfectly flat is a mystery I don't have time to contemplate.

"Ivan." He glances between us, reading the tension immediately. "Having trouble?"

I pull out the folded paper, wave it vaguely. "What do you get the Ursa King?"

There's a beat of silence.

Then Dristan says, absolutely deadpan: "A muzzle?"

Despite everything, I laugh. Actually, laugh. It's sharp and surprised and entirely inappropriate.

"Dristan!" Cassandra tries to sound scandalized, but she's fighting a smile.

"What? It's practical."

"Ivan." Cassandra drifts toward me and puts her hands on her hips. "Be nice. It's Christmas."

"It's MAY!"

The words echo off the high ceilings. A skull ornament swings gently on the tree.

"And," I continue, "you're asking me to buy a thoughtful gift for the man who branded you. Who kept Dristan away from you for months. Who made last Christmas—"

"Who's trying," she interrupts gently. Her hand finds my arm. "He's trying, Ivan. That's all I'm asking. From any of you. Just... try."

I look at her—six months pregnant, standing in a forest of Christmas decorations in the wrong season, asking me to extend compassion to someone who hurt her.

She's too good for all of us.

"You're impossible," I mutter.

"I'm pregnant and magical. I contain multitudes." She grins. "Now go shopping. Find something that acknowledges his effort without pretending everything's fine. Show him you see him trying."

"That's asking a lot."

"I know." Her expression softens. "But you'll figure it out. You always do."

Dristan, still holding his tangled lights, adds: "For what it's worth? Samara mentioned he's obsessed with smart home technology. Make of that what you will."

"Technology I can work with." I head for the door

again. "Emotion and forgiveness? Those are above my pay grade."

"Lucky for you," Cassandra calls after me, "Secret Santa only requires one of those things."

I pause at the threshold, looking back at them. Cassandra surrounded by decorations, one hand on her belly. Dristan watching her with that expression of fierce protectiveness mixed with adoration. Both of them trying so hard to build something good from the wreckage of last winter.

"Dristan," I say.

He looks up, eyebrows raised.

"Tomorrow evening. You're coming with me to find this gift."

"I am?"

"You suggested a muzzle. You're clearly invested in this disaster. And misery loves company."

"I have plans—"

"You're untangling Christmas lights," I point out. "Your *plans* are flexible."

Cassandra laughs, bright and delighted. "Oh, this is going to be fun."

"For you, maybe," I mutter, but I'm already planning the route. Champs-Élysées. The high-end tech district. Somewhere expensive enough to show respect, absurd enough to maintain dignity.

"Six o'clock," I tell Dristan. "Don't be late."

"I'm never late."

"You're *clearly* late in catching up with the season's fashion." I let my gaze sweep over his outfit with pointed disdain. "A cable-knit sweater in May?"

"That was Cassandra's doing," he grumbles.

"Six o'clock," I repeat, and step out into the Paris afternoon before either of them can rope me into more decoration duties.

Christmas in May.

This is going to be an unmitigated disaster.

I can't wait.

2

CASSANDRA: THE WHY

I wake to sunlight streaming through the bedroom windows and Dristan's cool hand on my very pregnant belly.

"It's moving," he murmurs, wonder in his voice like he hasn't said the exact same thing every morning for the past month.

"The baby has excellent timing," I say, not opening my eyes yet. "Always most active when I'm trying to sleep."

"Takes after its mother, then." His thumb traces gentle circles on my skin, and I feel the responding flutter of magic—mine, the baby's, impossibly intertwined. "Stubborn. Powerful. Determined to be noticed."

I crack one eye open. He's propped on his elbow beside me, hazel eyes fixed on my stomach with an expression of such naked adoration that my heart clenches. His ash blonde hair falls across his forehead, slightly mussed from sleep.

"You're staring again."

"I'm allowed to stare. It's a miracle."

"It's biology."

"It's *our* biology." He leans down to press a kiss just above my navel, where the baby kicks in response. "Our miracle. Our future."

I run my fingers through his hair, ash blonde and silky, catching the morning light. Three months since Gavriil's grief broke the brand. Three months of having Dristan back in my life without magical compulsion keeping us apart.

Three months of learning how to breathe again.

"What time is it?" I ask, though I already know. The sunlight has that specific quality—late morning, edging toward noon. I've slept in. Again.

"Nearly eleven." Dristan shifts to lie beside me properly, one arm draped protectively over my middle. "The party is tomorrow. You have today and part of tomorrow to finish destroying Juliette's manor and driving everyone insane with your festive cheer."

"*Our* manor," I correct automatically. "Grand-mère inherited it to me, remember? So it's ours now. Though not for much longer."

"Counting down the days until Saint-Germain-des-Prés?" His voice warms with anticipation. "Ten more days until the renovations are finished."

"Ten days," I repeat, smiling. "Our own place. No

Grand-mère hovering. No Ivan, making sardonic commentary about my decorating choices. Just us."

"And the baby."

"And the baby." I press my hand over his. "I can't wait. The nursery you designed is perfect. The library with the reading nook. That kitchen with actual counter space."

"The bedroom with the balcony overlooking the courtyard." His eyes darken with promise. "Privacy. Finally."

"I love Juliette, but—"

"But you want to be able to have loud sex without vampire hearing picking up every sound?"

I laugh, swatting his shoulder. "I was going to say, 'but I want our own space to build our life together,' but yes, that too."

"The painters finished the nursery yesterday," Dristan says, tracing patterns on my belly. "I went by to check. The stars on the ceiling glow exactly as you wanted. Soft enough not to overstimulate, bright enough to comfort."

"You're going to be such a good father."

Something flickers across his face—vulnerability, fear, hope all tangled together. "I want to be. I want to give this child everything. You. A home. A family. Safety."

"You already are." I cup his face, making him look at me. "You're here. You're present. You're preparing our home with such care and love. That's everything."

He leans into my touch. "Sometimes I still can't believe I'm here. That I get to have this. You. The baby. A future. Our own place to make a life together."

My chest tightens. "Dristan—"

"When Gavriil's brand forced me away last winter, I thought—" He stops. Swallows. "I thought I'd lost you. Lost this. Lost everything."

"But you didn't." I press my forehead to his. "You came back. The brand is broken. We're together."

"We're together," he repeats, like a promise. Like a prayer.

We lie there in silence for a moment, just breathing. Just existing together.

This. This is why I need tomorrow to be perfect.

"It's Christmas," I say finally.

Dristan blinks. "It's May."

"It's Christmas *enough*." I sit up—a process that now requires strategic maneuvering and mild levitation magic. "And I'm throwing a party. A real one. With everyone we love. Because last Christmas—"

I stop.

Dristan sits up too, instantly alert. "Cassandra."

"Last Christmas was horrible."

"I know."

"No, you don't." The words come out sharper than I intend. "You weren't here for it. You couldn't be, because of the—" I gesture vaguely at my arm, where Gavriil's brand used to burn. Where it still sometimes aches phantom-like in my nightmares. "Because of the spell. The binding. All of it."

"Tell me," he says quietly.

I don't want to. I've spent months trying *not* to think about last December. About being trapped in this manor, branded and powerless, while Dristan was magically compelled to stay away.

About spending Christmas Eve alone.

But maybe that's the problem. Maybe I need to say it out loud. Exorcise the memory by speaking it into existence.

"I woke up on Christmas morning," I begin, staring at my hands, "and for a few seconds, I forgot. Forgot about the brand. Forgot about Gavriil's binding spell. Forgot that you couldn't be here."

The memory surfaces with crystalline clarity.

December 25th. Last year.

I wake to silence.

That's the first wrong thing. Christmas morning should be loud—Juliette playing Baroque carols on the antique phonograph, Ivan complaining about the noise, the smell of something burning because someone inevitably tries to cook.

But there's nothing. Just the hollow quiet of the manor and the winter wind against the windows.

I touch my left forearm instinctively. The brand burns—Gavriil's mark, the Ursa King's claim, the magical binding that's trapped me here for three weeks now. Three weeks of him slowly breaking me down, teaching me to use the power he forced on me, reshaping my magic into something I barely recognize.

Three weeks since Dristan had to leave.

Had to. The spell compels him. Gavriil engineered it perfectly. Keep me isolated. Keep me dependent. Keep me his.

I'm so gods-damned tired of being kept.

I haul myself out of bed—slower now, the pregnancy making everything harder. Eight weeks along. Barely showing. I shouldn't be able to feel the baby moving; even so, I sense it. Restless, as if it knows something is wrong.

The manor is decorated. Juliette insisted, even though she's away from home, dealing with some vampire political crisis. Even though Ivan is with her. Even though I begged them not to leave me alone.

"You're not alone," Juliette had said, kissing my forehead. "Gavriil will check on you."

As if that's comfort. As if my jailer checking on me makes imprisonment more bearable.

I wander downstairs in my nightgown and robe. The Christmas tree stands in the parlor—elegant, perfectly decorated, mocking me with its cheer. Presents underneath, wrapped in silver and black.

None from Dristan.

I sit on the floor in front of the tree—undignified, pregnant, pathetic—and I cry.

Not delicate tears. Ugly, gasping sobs that shake my whole body. The baby's magic stirs frantically, responding to my distress, and my magic flares wild and violet, making the tree lights flicker and pop.

I'm alone.

On Christmas.

Branded.

Trapped.

Pregnant with a child whose father I can never speak to again.

And the worst part? The absolute worst part?

Last night, I dreamt of Dristan. His voice—strained, careful, trying so hard to sound normal—revealed agony underneath. Even dreaming of him hurts now. Even hearing his voice triggers the brand's punishment.

"I love you," he'd said, words clipped short.

And then silence.

The doorbell rings.

I ignore it.

It rings again. Insistent.

Fine. Whatever. Maybe it's a delivery. Maybe it's someone who'll actually help break this damn spell.

I open the door.

Gavriil Alexeev stands on my doorstep, massive and imposing in a black coat, snow dusting his shoulders. His dark eyes take in my tear-stained face, my disheveled hair, my obvious breakdown.

"Merry Christmas, printsessa," he says in that low Russian rumble.

I want to slam the door in his face. Want to curse him in three languages. Want to summon enough magic to blast him off my property.

Instead, I dissolve into tears again.

Because this is my Christmas. This is what my life has become.

The Ursa King who branded me and drove away the man I love is the only person who bothered to show up.

"He stayed," I tell Dristan now, back in the present,

in our bedroom, in the light. "All day. Didn't talk much. Just... stayed. Made sure I ate. Fixed the tree lights I'd blown out with my crying. Sat in the library reading while I slept on the couch because I couldn't bear to be alone anymore."

Dristan's jaw is tight. "Cassandra—"

"I'm not saying I forgive him." I need him to understand this. "The brand. The binding spell. Keeping you away from me, making every interaction between us agony—that's not erased by one day of basic human decency."

"Then why invite him?"

"Because he *stayed*." The words burst out of me, raw and true. "When everyone else had a reason to be somewhere else—even Grand-mère, even Ivan—when you literally couldn't be near me, he stayed. And later, albeit unknowingly, he gave me his grief to break the spell. To bring Luciana back and free us both."

I turn to face Dristan fully. "And because tomorrow is about rewriting that memory. Last Christmas, I was alone and broken and trapped. You were in agony, forced to stay away. *This* Christmas—"

"It's May."

"This Christmas," I continue, ignoring him, "everyone I love is here. You're here—really here, without pain, without magical compulsion keeping us apart. Juliette is here. Ivan is here. Gavriil and Luciana are together again. Samara and Nikolaas are actually trying to beat the Draken curse. Clarissa and Kaisner survived the Mahindras. Vlad gets to see his family.

We're all *here*. And in ten days, we move into our own home. Our real beginning."

My magic rises with my emotion, violet flames dancing at my fingertips. The baby kicks hard, responding to my power.

"I need this party to be perfect," I say. "Not because I care about the decorations or the food or whether anyone actually likes their Secret Santa gift. But because I need to prove to myself that we made it. That we survived. That happiness is possible even after everything we've been through. That we get to have this—this life, this family, this future."

"Even if it's May?"

"*Especially* because it's May." I grab his hand, press it to my belly where our child moves. "Timing doesn't matter. Calendar dates don't matter. What matters is that we're together and we get to celebrate that. Right now. Christmas in May, because I say so."

Dristan stares at me for a long moment. Then he starts to laugh.

"What?" I demand.

"You," he says, pulling me close—as close as the baby allows. "You're magnificent. Absolutely insane, but magnificent."

"I'm hormonal and magical and determined. It's a devastating combination."

"I *am* aware." He kisses me, soft and reverent. "And you're right. About all of it. It will be perfect because we'll make it perfect. Christmas in May, gothic decorations, Secret Santa disasters, and all."

"Even the ugly Christmas sweater?"

He pulls back, suspicious. "What ugly Christmas sweater?"

I gesture to the chair in the corner, where a truly spectacular black and red monstrosity hangs. It features a vampire Santa, complete with fangs, holding a "Naughty List" with blood dripping from the letters.

Dristan stares at it in horror. "No."

"You promised."

"I promised no such thing."

"You said, and I quote, 'Whatever you need to make tomorrow special.'"

"That was in a moment of passion! You were using your feminine wiles!"

"And they worked." I'm grinning now, the darkness of the memory finally lifting. "You're wearing it."

"I'm a millenary vampire."

"You're *my* millenary vampire. And you're wearing the sweater."

We lock eyes. I see the moment he surrenders.

"You're impossible," he mutters.

"You love me."

"Unfortunately." But he's smiling, reaching for the monstrosity. "This is what I get for falling in love with a witch. Emotional manipulation and terrible fashion choices."

"Don't forget the pregnancy hormones."

"How could I?" He pulls the sweater on over his head. It fits perfectly—because of course, I used magic to ensure it would. The vampire Santa leers from his chest, gloriously tacky against his ash blonde hair.

He looks absolutely ridiculous—*very* handsomely so.

He also looks happy.

"Perfect," I say, snapping a photo with my phone.

"You're not posting that."

"I'm *definitely* posting that."

"Cassandra—"

"It's Christmas, babe. Time to spread the joy." I pull myself out of bed—less gracefully than I'd like—and head for the closet. "Now, I need to get dressed. We have a tree to finish decorating, a feast to prepare, and approximately thirty hours before our family arrives to witness our complete descent into holiday madness."

"Thirty hours," Dristan repeats, still wearing the sweater, looking at himself in the mirror with resignation. "This is really happening."

He meets my eyes in the reflection. "For what it's worth? I'm glad. Not about the sweater—"

"Obviously."

"—but about today. About you reclaiming this. Rewriting the memory. Taking back your joy. And in ten days, we'll have our own place to make even more memories. Good ones."

My throat tightens. "Saint-Germain-des-Prés. Our home."

"Our home," he confirms. "With the nursery I spent a month designing. The kitchen where you can experiment with witch recipes without Juliette's commentary. The library where we can read together while the baby sleeps. Our beginning."

"Thank you," I whisper. "For understanding. For being here. For building us a life. For—" I gesture vaguely at the sweater. "All of it."

"Where else would I be?" He crosses to me, takes my face in his hands. "You broke the brand, Cassandra. You brought Luciana back and freed us both. The least I can do is wear a ridiculous sweater and help you throw Christmas in May."

I kiss him, long and deep and grateful.

"I love you," I whisper against his lips.

"I love you too, baby." He rests his forehead against mine.

"Even when I'm completely insane?"

"That's when I love you most."

We stand there for a moment, just breathing together. Then the baby kicks—hard—and we both laugh.

"Your child is demanding breakfast," Dristan observes.

"*Our* child is demanding breakfast. And probably Christmas cookies."

"It's eleven in the morning."

"It's Christmas. Christmas rules apply."

"It's May."

"*Christmas rules apply.*"

He sighs in defeat. "I'll make the cookies. You finish getting dressed. Try not to levitate anything too heavy—doctor's orders."

"The doctor also said I should avoid stress."

"And yet you're throwing a dinner party for thirteen supernatural beings, complete with Secret Santa and gothic decorations."

"Exactly. Very calming. Very demure. Very zen."

"You enjoy my suffering."

"Immensely."

He heads downstairs, ugly Christmas sweater and all, and I watch him go with warmth spreading through my chest. For the first time since last December, Christmas doesn't hurt. It feels like hope.

Like joy reclaimed from darkness.

And in ten days, we'll have our own home. Our own space to build the life we fought so hard for.

I pull on black maternity jeans and a flowing silver top that accommodates the baby bump. Add the snowflake fuzzy socks because why not. Twist my hair up with the candy cane pencil because commitment to the aesthetic is important.

Look at myself in the mirror.

Pregnant. Powerful. Happy.

Free.

"Okay, baby," I murmur, pressing my hand to my belly. "Let's set up the most ridiculous Christmas party in supernatural history."

The baby kicks in what I choose to interpret as agreement.

I head downstairs to the smell of cookies baking and the sound of Dristan arguing with the oven—"It's not supposed to smoke, Cassandra! Ovens don't just *smoke!*"—and I laugh.

This. This is what I needed last Christmas.

This is what I'm celebrating today.

Life. Love. Family. Joy. Freedom.

Christmas doesn't need a calendar.

It just needs us.

3

DRISTAN: FIRST CHRISTMAS

I'm standing in the kitchen of Deveraux Manor, wearing an ugly Christmas sweater in May, attempting to convince an oven that it should cooperate, when I realize something profound:

I'm happy.

Not content. Not merely satisfied. *Happy*. The kind of bone-deep joy I haven't felt in... centuries? Longer?

The oven beeps indignantly, and smoke pours from the edges of the door.

"Bloody hell." I wave a dish towel at the smoke detector before it can trigger. The cookies inside are supposed to be golden brown, not charcoal black. "Cassandra? The oven is possessed!"

"It's not possessed!" Her voice drifts down from upstairs, amused. "You probably set it too high again!"

"I set it exactly where the recipe indicated."

"The recipe assumes you're using Celsius, not Fahrenheit!"

Ah. That would explain it.

I adjust the temperature and pull out the tray of blackened disasters. They were supposed to be snowflake-shaped sugar cookies. They're now snowflake-shaped carbon deposits.

"Take two," I mutter, reaching for more dough.

The thing is—I don't mind. Not really. Burned cookies, temperamental ovens, ugly Christmas sweaters in entirely the wrong season—it's all absurdly, perfectly mundane.

And mundane is a gift.

Five months ago, I couldn't come close to this manor without experiencing pain so intense it felt like my bones were splintering. Gavriil's brand saw to that. Physical agony for both of us. Magical torment designed to keep us apart.

I'd tried once. Only once.

December 25. Christmas Day.

I stand outside Deveraux Manor at midnight, staring at the windows where I know Cassandra sleeps. Or tries to sleep. I don't even know she's pregnant with our child, and I haven't been able to touch her in weeks.

Weeks since Gavriil Alexeev branded her. Weeks of magical compulsion keeping me at a distance. The longest weeks of hell.

I take a step toward the door.

Pain explodes through my chest—white-hot, excruciating, like someone's driving iron spikes through my sternum. I gasp, doubling over, and inside the manor, I hear Cassandra scream.

She's feeling it too. The brand punishes us both, though I don't understand it at the time.

I stagger back, the pain receding to a dull throb. My hands shake. My vision blurs.

Inside, Cassandra is sobbing. I can hear her even from here, my vampire senses picking up every broken sound. Cassandra's magic flares wild and violet, making the windows rattle.

Somehow, I did that. My proximity caused her that pain.

Gavriil appears in the doorway. He doesn't speak. Doesn't need to. His dark eyes say everything: Leave. You're hurting her. You can't be here.

I leave.

I leave her alone, pregnant, terrified, during Christmas.

I leave because staying would only cause more pain.

I hate myself for it.

The memory still burns like acid. I'd spent Christmas Day in my manor in Montparnasse, alone, clutching my phone, wanting desperately to call her but knowing that even my voice would cause her distress. The brand's magic was that thorough. That cruel.

The second batch of cookies is taking shape now—proper golden brown, edges just crisp enough. I'm learning. Adapting. Like everything else in this new life we're building.

"How's it going down there?" Cassandra appears in the doorway, radiant in silver and black, one hand on her pregnant belly. She's glowing. Literally glowing with magic and happiness, and that particular quality unique to her.

"Better," I say, pulling out the tray. Perfect this time. "Only minor disasters. Nothing I couldn't handle."

"That's my millenary vampire." She crosses to me, wrapping her arms around my waist from behind, resting her cheek against the ridiculous sweater. "My competent, patient, slightly-too-tall-for-this-kitchen love."

I turn in her embrace, careful not to jostle her belly. "Compliments won't make me forget you convinced me to wear this monstrosity."

"The sweater makes you look approachable."

"I'm a vampire. I'm not supposed to be approachable."

"You're about to be a father. Approachable is mandatory." She grins up at me, violet flames flickering in her storm-grey eyes. "Besides, you look adorable."

"I look ridiculous."

"Adorably ridiculous."

I kiss her because I can. Because there's no pain now. No magical compulsion. No brand keeping us apart. Just her, me, and the life growing between us.

"I love you," I murmur against her lips.

"I love you too." She pulls back, studying my face. "You're thinking about last Christmas."

It's not a question. She knows me too well.

"Hard not to," I admit. "Being here. Doing this. It's everything I wanted then and couldn't have."

"But you have it now."

"I have it now." I touch her face, tracing the line of her cheekbone. "You. The baby. This absurd party. Our home in Saint-Germain-des-Prés waiting for us. All of it."

"Ten more days," she says softly. "Ten days and we're in our own space. No more Juliette commentary. No more Ivan's sardonic observations. Just us."

"I'm still finishing the nursery details." I can't help the pride that creeps into my voice. "The rocking chair arrived yesterday. Antique, eighteenth-century, reupholstered in that soft grey fabric you liked. And the mobile—the one with the fairies, the silver stars, and crescent moons—it's hung perfectly above the crib."

"You're nesting."

"I'm *preparing*."

"You're nesting." She's laughing now, delighted. "My ancient vampire is nesting like an expectant mother."

"I prefer 'thoughtfully anticipating our child's arrival.'"

"Nesting."

I sigh, but I'm smiling too. "Fine. I'm nesting. But in a very masculine, vampire-appropriate way."

"Of course. Very intimidating nest-building." She steals a cookie from the cooling rack, bites into it. Her eyes close in pleasure. "These are perfect. You're getting good at this domestic thing."

"I've had nearly a thousand years to perfect various skills. Baking was simply... previously unnecessary."

"And now?"

"Now it matters." I watch her eat the cookie, memorizing every detail. The way she licks sugar from her bottom lip. The contented hum she makes. The protective hand she keeps on her belly. "Everything matters now. Cookies, Christmas parties in May, ugly sweaters. Because it's ours. Because we get to have this."

Her expression softens. "You really love it, don't you? The ordinary moments."

"I love all of it." The words come out more intense than I intend, but they're true. Raw truth. "Last winter, I couldn't touch you. I couldn't be in the same room. Couldn't hear your voice without the brand punishing us. And now—" I gesture at the kitchen, at the cookies, at her. "Now I get to burn cookies in your grandmother's kitchen while wearing a ridiculous sweater, and it's the most precious thing I've ever experienced."

Cassandra's eyes shimmer with unshed tears. "Dristan—"

"I know why you're doing this," I continue. "The party. Christmas in May. All of it. You're reclaiming what was stolen. Taking back joy from the pain. But Cassandra—" I pull her close, one hand on her belly, feeling our child move beneath my palm. "You gave me back more than you realize. Not just access to you. Not just freedom from the brand. You gave me a reason to care about burned cookies and holiday parties, and building nurseries. You gave me a life worth living."

A tear escapes, rolling down her cheek. "I love you so much it terrifies me sometimes."

"Good." I brush the tear away with my thumb. "Love should be a little terrifying. Means it matters."

The baby kicks against my hand—hard enough that we both feel it.

"Someone agrees," Cassandra says, laughing through her tears. "Or someone wants more cookies."

"Both, probably." I kiss her forehead. "Go sit down. I'll finish the baking. You're supposed to be resting."

"I'm pregnant, not fragile."

"You're pregnant with unprecedented magical power while planning a party for thirteen supernatural beings. Humor me."

She narrows her eyes. "Fine. But only because these socks are really comfortable and I want to put my feet up."

I watch her waddle—and it is a waddle now, though I'd never say it aloud—to the breakfast nook, where she settles into the cushioned bench with a satisfied sigh.

"Thank you," she says quietly. "For understanding. For being here. For making cookies and wearing ugly sweaters and just... showing up for this."

"Where else would I be?"

"I don't know. Most vampires would find this beneath them. Domestic. Boring."

"Most vampires haven't spent months being magically barred from the person they love." I turn back to the cookies, arranging them on a decorative platter. "Most vampires don't know what it's like to lose something this precious and get it back. I don't take a single moment for granted, Cassandra. Not one."

For a moment, neither of us speaks. The kitchen settles into a soothing warmth, a feeling born of shared understanding.

"Do you remember your last real Christmas?" she suddenly asks. "Before you were turned?"

"I remember *one* Christmas. I was twenty. My family's estate in Wessex. My mother insisted on attending midnight mass despite the snow. My father complained about the cold. My sisters argued over who got to wear Mother's good cloak."

"Were you happy?"

"I thought I was." I arrange the last cookie, then turn to face her. "But it was surface happiness. Expected happiness. I played the role of dutiful eldest son. Smiled at the right moments. Said the right things. But I didn't feel it. Not really."

"And now?"

"Now?" I look at her—pregnant, powerful, surrounded by her chaotic Christmas plans, planning our future in Saint-Germain-des-Prés. "Now I feel everything. And it's terrifying and wonderful and so much more than I ever had when I was mortal."

She smiles, and it's the sun breaking through clouds. "Good. Because I need you to feel everything. All the chaos. All the awkwardness. All the ridiculousness of Christmas in May. I need you to be present for it."

"I'm not going anywhere." I cross over to her, sit beside her in the breakfast nook. "Though I reserve the right to make sardonic comments when things inevitably go wrong."

"Oh, things will absolutely go wrong." She leans her head on my shoulder. "Gavriil will be awkward. Ivan will be judgmental and cranky. Someone will definitely set something on fire."

"Probably one of the dragons," I say. "Volatile tempers."

"Exactly." Cassandra laces her fingers through mine. "But you know what? Even if it all goes horribly wrong, it'll still be better than last Christmas. Because we'll be together. Because you're here."

"I'm here," I confirm, squeezing her hand. "I'm here for every moment. The disasters, the joy, the Gothic Christmas decorations in the wrong season. All of it."

We sit there in comfortable silence, her head on my shoulder, my hand on her belly, cookies cooling on the counter, ugly sweater and all.

This is what I wanted last Christmas. What I dreamed about during those agonizing weeks of separation.

Not grand gestures. Not dramatic declarations.

Just this. Just her. Just us.

The ordinary, extraordinary miracle of being together.

"We should probably finish decorating," Cassandra says eventually. "And I need to start on the feast. And there's still the matter of the gift bags—"

"One step at a time." I kiss the top of her head. "We

have all day. And now, I get to help. No pain. No brand. No magical compulsion keeping me away."

"No pain," she echoes softly. "Just us."

Just us. And really, that's all the Christmas miracle I need.

Even if it is May.

Because timing doesn't matter when you've learned what it's like to lose everything and get it back.

What matters is that we're here. Together. Building a life. Making memories.

Burning cookies and wearing ugly sweaters and planning our future in a home that's ours.

This is everything.

And I won't take a single moment for granted.

4

GAVRIIL: PENANCE

I stare at the invitation on my desk, black cardstock with silver lettering, and I want to throw it in the fire.

A Very Supernatural Christmas (in May). Deveraux Manor Saturday, 6 PM. Festive attire encouraged.

Christmas. In May.

Only Cassandra Deveraux would do something this absurd.

Only Cassandra Deveraux would invite the man who branded her against her will to celebrate anything at all.

"You're brooding again," Luciana says from the doorway of my study. She's wearing a simple white dress, her blonde hair loose around her shoulders, dreamy eyes—violet since her resurrection—studying me with that knowing look.

"Я не впадаю в уныние." *I'm not brooding*, I mutter in Russian. "I'm considering our options."

"Our options are: go to the party, or insult the witch who brought me back from the dead." Luciana crosses the room, perches on the edge of my desk. "Not much of a choice, Daddy Bear."

I grunt. The nickname—her weapon when she wants something from me. And she's right, of course. She's always right.

Five months since the winter solstice. Since Cassandra cast the resurrection spell on the longest night of the year. But only three months since I learned the truth—that the brand, the magical binding I'd forced on Cassandra at the Yule Ball, had served as a conduit. My grief for Luciana, channeled through that bracelet into Cassandra's power. Three months since she told me Luciana was alive.

I hadn't known. Hadn't understood what I was giving her.

But ignorance doesn't absolve me.

"She invited us," I say, still staring at the invitation. "After everything I did to her. She invited us to *Christmas*." I pause, bemused. "Is this a political ploy?"

"Oh, my love. You've been Ursa King too long." Luciana picks up the invitation, examines it with a slight smile. "She's making a point. She's saying: I survived. I'm happy. I'm celebrating. And you're invited because I choose to invite you."

"It's May."

"So?"

"Christmas is in December."

Luciana laughs, that bright sound I went a year without hearing. A year of grief and darkness and thinking I'd lost her forever. "Gavriil Alexeev. Ursa King. Alpha of the Russian bear shifter community, authority recognized worldwide. Complaining about the timing of a holiday party."

"It's absurd."

"It's wonderful." She sets the invitation down, cups my face with her hands. Small hands. Delicate. Strong. "She's reclaiming joy. Taking back what happened to her last Christmas."

The words land harder than I expect.

Last Christmas. When Cassandra had been alone in Deveraux Manor, branded, trapped, pregnant, and terrified. When the millenary vampire had been forced away by the spell's compulsion. When Juliette and Ivan were away.

When I was the only one who showed up.

December 25. Last year.

I arrive at Deveraux Manor with no real plan. Just an awareness that Cassandra is alone. That it's Christmas. That despite everything—the brand, the binding, the complicated mess of power and politics between us—leaving her completely alone feels... wrong.

She answers the door in a nightgown and robe, hair disheveled, face tear-stained.

"Merry Christmas, printsessa," I say, because what else is there to say?

She stares at me. Then bursts into tears.

I stand there, massive and useless, while she sobs. The Ursa King, leader of my people, completely helpless in the face of a crying witch.

"I'm sorry," I finally manage. "I can leave—"

"No." The word comes out choked. "Don't. Please don't."

So I don't.

I stay. All day. Don't talk much—what would I say? The brand keeps the millenary vampire away. Keeps her isolated. I did what was necessary for my clan, for both our families —the alliance we needed. But standing here, watching her sob on Christmas morning, necessary feels hollow.

I fix the Christmas lights that she's blown out with her power surge. Make sure she eats something. Sit in the library reading while she sleeps on the couch, exhausted and pregnant, and alone.

It's the least I can do.

It's nowhere near enough.

"You're thinking about last Christmas," Luciana observes, her hands still on my face.

"How can I not?" I pull away, stand, pace to the window. Our manor in the 16th arrondissement overlooks a private garden. Spring has arrived—flowers blooming, trees green, completely wrong for Christmas. "I branded her, Luciana. Forced a magical bond on her without consent. Kissed her at the Yule Ball and marked her as mine when she belonged to no one but herself."

"I know."

"I kept the millenary vampire away. Made every interaction between them agony. Left her isolated and dependent on me." I turn to face her. "I did what I thought was right. For my clan. For the alliance between our families. But right now—" I gesture at the invitation. "Standing here now, knowing what it cost her—"

"I know," Luciana repeats, firmer now. She stands, crosses to me. "When I came back, the brand bracelet was still there. She told me everything, Gavriil. In the garden. What the brand did to her. The pain. The agony of being apart from her beloved Dristan. How her magic was forcibly reshaped. How she spent Christmas alone because of what you did."

The words settle in my chest like stones.

"I saw the fear in her eyes when she looked at it," Luciana continues quietly. "The bracelet. She'll never forget what it meant."

"Then you understand why I can't go to this party. Why seeing me would ruin her Christmas. Why—"

"Why you're afraid." She takes my hand, places it over her heart. I feel the steady beat beneath my palm. Alive. Real. Back after a year of emptiness. "You're afraid she'll look at you and remember only the pain. Afraid the millenary vampire will attack you. Afraid you'll never be anything but the villain in their story."

I don't answer. Can't.

"But she invited you anyway," Luciana continues softly. "Knowing all of that. She invited you. And me. To celebrate."

"I don't deserve—"

"Of course you don't." She squeezes my hand. "But

you gave her this. Through that spell, through that bracelet, through your grief—you gave her the power to bring me back. To break the brand. To free herself and the millenary vampire."

"I didn't know I was doing it."

"Does that matter?"

"Yes!" The word comes out louder than I intend. "Intent matters. I branded her to secure an alliance. To bind her power to mine. To ensure our families' survival. The fact that it accidentally gave her something useful doesn't erase my reasons for doing it."

Luciana studies me for a long moment. Then: "No. It doesn't erase it. You did what you thought you had to do. For your people. But Gavriil—" She squeezes my hand. "You can't undo the past. You can only choose what you do now. And right now, Cassandra Deveraux is giving you a choice: stay in your guilt, or show up for her celebration."

"She doesn't want me there. She's being polite."

"You're wrong." Luciana's voice is certain. "I've spoken with her. Twice, since... since I came back. She's hurt, yes. But she's also grateful. For this." She gestures to herself. "For me. And she's trying, Gavriil. Trying to build something new. To move forward."

"By throwing Christmas in May."

"By refusing to let trauma define her." Luciana's violet eyes flash. "She could have spent the rest of her life hating you. Avoiding you. Making everyone choose sides. Instead, she's inviting you to celebrate. She's saying: what happened, happened. But we're all still here. Still alive. Still family."

Family.

Guilt claws at my ribs, impossible to shake.

I think of Samara, still living here in the manor with us. Not yet twenty-one—too young by witch standards to be on her own, though she's trying so hard to build a life with Nikolaas, anyway. She's been patient with me these past months, with my moods, with the complicated dance of having Luciana back while still carrying the burden of what I did to Cassandra.

"Vlad and Anya are coming," Luciana adds, practical now. "Your brother wants to see you. And little Katya—Gavriil, she's walking now. Talking. You haven't seen her since she was born."

Another twist of guilt. I've been so focused on my own complications with Cassandra, on adjusting to having Luciana back, that I've neglected my actual family.

"Samara's hoping you'll be there too," Luciana continues. "She told me yesterday. She misses having her brother around, not just the Ursa King brooding in his study."

My sister. Who stood by me through everything. Who's still here under my roof, still believing I can be better than I've been.

"And you drew Cassandra's name," Luciana says, almost casually.

I freeze. "What?"

"For Secret Santa. I drew for you when I visited her

last week—you got Cassandra." Luciana's smile is mischievous now. "Which means you need to give her a gift. Face to face."

"No."

"Yes."

"I can't—what do you even give—"

"That's your problem to solve." She kisses my cheek, then heads for the door. "We're going, Daddy Bear. I'm not missing my first Christmas since my return—even if it is in May—because you're too stubborn to accept forgiveness when it's offered."

She's gone before I can argue.

I sink back into my chair, staring at the invitation.

Secret Santa.

I have to give Cassandra a gift.

The woman I branded. The woman whose last Christmas I helped ruin, even if my intentions were for the greater good.

What do you give someone you've hurt?

"An apology," I mutter to myself. "Though that's hardly gift-wrapping material."

But Luciana's right. She's always right.

I can't undo what I did. Can't take back the brand, the binding, the pain. The choices I made for my people, for our families, that cost Cassandra so dearly. Can't erase the memory of her sobbing on Christmas morning because I was the only person who showed up.

But I can show up now. Again. Not as her captor. Not as the Ursa King asserting dominance.

As someone trying to make amends. Failing, probably. But trying.

I pull out my phone, text Samara:

> What does one give a pregnant witch for Christmas in May?

Her response is immediate:

> Your presence, brother. She doesn't want a gift. She wants you to show up.

Then, a moment later:

> But also maybe something thoughtful. Not expensive. Meaningful.

I stare at the phone.

Meaningful.

What's meaningful to Cassandra?

Family. Magic. Books. History. Control over her power.

And then it hits me.

I know exactly what to give her.

I stand, grab my jacket. I have shopping to do.

And a party to attend.

5

GAVRIIL: TRY NOT TO TERRIFY THE CHILD

T hree hours later, after combing through half the bookshops in Paris, I find Cassandra's gift in a small antiquarian shop in the Latin Quarter. Antique, leather-bound, pages yellowed with age. Back at the manor, I carefully set it on my desk and read the cover engraved in gold:

Grimoire de la Resurrection et de la Vie

A 17th-century grimoire on resurrection magic and life force manipulation. Rare. Powerful. Exactly the kind of thing Cassandra would treasure.

But more than that—it's a grimoire she can use. Study. Master. Take control of the power that was forced on her through my brand.

Knowledge. Agency. Choice.

The things the brand took from her.

The things she's fought to reclaim.

I'm wrapping the grimoire in simple black paper when footsteps approach my study.

"Gavriil."

I know that voice. Know the particular cadence of it, the easy confidence that's both infuriating and admirable in equal measure.

Vlad leans against the doorframe, arms crossed, looking entirely too amused for someone who just flew in from Saint Petersburg. He's wearing dark jeans and a leather jacket—casual in that way only wolves can pull off, making it look effortless rather than careless.

"Brother," I acknowledge, not looking up from the ribbon I'm attempting to tie. It's not cooperating. Ribbons never cooperate with bear shifters. Our hands are too large, too blunt for delicate work.

"I heard you're actually coming to this circus." He pushes off the doorframe, enters uninvited. Typical Vlad. "Luciana's work, I assume?"

"She insists."

"Luciana is wise." He picks up the invitation from my desk, examines it with that critical eye he usually reserves for pack negotiations. "Christmas in May. Only Cassandra Deveraux would attempt something this absurd."

"Agreed."

"And yet, we're *all* going." He sets the invitation down, turns that silver gaze on me. Our father's eyes, even if we don't share blood. The Alexeev line runs true. "Says something about her, doesn't it? That she can convince all of us to participate in her madness."

I grunt noncommittally, finally giving up on the ribbon and leaving it in a lopsided bow. Good enough.

Vlad crosses the room, picks up the loose ribbon ends without asking permission. His fingers work the silk with ease—quick, efficient movements that somehow result in a perfect bow.

"Anya makes me wrap all of Katya's gifts," he says, as if this explains everything. "Says it builds character."

"Does it?"

"It builds resentment toward ribbon manufacturers." But he's smiling as he steps back, examining his work. "There. Now it looks like you actually care."

"I do care."

"I know." He settles into the chair across from my desk, that easy wolf grace making even sitting look effortless. "That's why you've been brooding in here instead of just refusing to go."

His smile turns fond.

"Anya and Katya are here," Vlad says, and something in his tone shifts. Less casual. More weighted.

I look up then. "Your daughter is—what, a year now?"

"Fourteen months." The correction is immediate, precise. The way all new parents track time. "Walking everywhere. Talking in two-word sentences—mostly demanding things in Russian. 'Papa up.' 'Mama cookie.' 'Snow now.'" He shakes his head, but there's pride in his expression. Pure, undiluted pride. "And her magic... Gavriil, she's already showing signs of being a wolf-witch hybrid. Yesterday, she made it snow in the nursery because she was excited about a story Anya was reading. The day before, she turned her stuffed bear blue because she wanted it to match her blanket."

Despite myself, I feel the corner of my mouth twitch. "Sounds like a handful."

"She's everything." The answer is simple, but the significance behind is profound. "We're bringing Katya to the party." He pauses, his expression grows serious. "Try not to terrify the child."

It hits harder than I'm ready for.

"I don't terrify children."

"Gavriil." Vlad's laugh is short, sharp. "You terrify everyone. It's your gift. You walk into a room, and people calculate exit routes. You speak, and alphas reconsider their life choices. You exist with the permanent energy of someone who might throw you through a wall if you breathe wrong."

"I don't—"

"You do." But there's no malice in his voice. Just truth, stated plainly. "Daddy Bear. That's what Luciana calls you, and it's accurate. You're protective and powerful and absolutely terrifying to anyone who doesn't know you're all bluster and Russian stoicism."

"I'm not all bluster."

"No. Sometimes you're actual violence." He grins. "But my point stands. Katya is fourteen months old.

She's sensitive. Her magic responds to emotions—fear, joy, anger, all of it. And she'll be walking into a room full of tension and old wounds and supernatural beings who are all pretending to be fine while holding grudges that predate her existence by centuries."

I think about that. A toddler. A wolf-witch whose power reacts to the emotional atmosphere around her. Walking into Cassandra's party, where the undercurrents run deep and dangerous. Where Ivan will watch me with barely concealed hostility. Where Nikolaas and Kaisner might actually kill each other over dragon politics. Where Cassandra herself might see me and remember pain. Where I'll have to give her a gift and hope she doesn't throw it—and me—out.

"Anya's worried," Vlad continues, quieter now. "Not about Cassandra. Cassandra will be fine. She'll probably shower Katya with attention and magic and make her feel like the most special cub in the world. But the others..." He trails off. "Your presence at this party matters, Gavriil. Not just to Cassandra. To me. To Samara. To our family. But if you show up radiating Ursa King authority and making everyone feel like they're about to be judged..."

"Katya will sense it."

"Katya will sense it. And then we'll have a fourteen-month-old having feelings, which means weather phenomena or accidental transfiguration or—who knows? She made flowers grow in February because she was happy. What happens when she's scared?"

I sink back in my chair, the wrapped grimoire

sitting between us like an accusation. "I'll be civil," I say.

"You're always civil. That's not the same as being warm." Vlad moves closer, rests his hands on my desk. "Katya is your niece, Gavriil. Your brother's daughter. The future of our combined bloodline—Alexeev and Volkov. She should know her uncle as more than the stern Ursa King who shows up at pack meetings and intimidates everyone into submission."

The words sit heavy in my chest. I think about Samara, who I've been so focused on protecting that I've forgotten to simply be her brother. About Vlad, whom I haven't seen in months. About family—real family, not pack dynamics or political alliances—and how I've let my guilt over Cassandra consume everything else.

"I'm not good with children," I admit.

"Neither was our father." Vlad's grin is sharp, knowing. "And look how we turned out. One of us rules the Russian bear shifter community with an iron fist wrapped in diplomatic paperwork. The other built a pack from nothing and proved every wolf who rejected him wrong. We did alright for a couple of cubs raised by a bear with the emotional range of a glacier."

Despite everything, I almost smile.

"Father would have killed you for that comment."

"He tried. Multiple times." Vlad straightens. "But he also loved us, in his way. Showed us what it meant to be strong. To protect our people. To make the hard choices." He pauses. "You're doing that now, Gavriil.

Making the hard choice to show up, to face what you've done, to try. That's worth something."

"Is it?"

"Ask Luciana." He heads for the door, then pauses at the threshold. "Come to the party, brother. Be uncomfortable. Be awkward. Radiate Ursa King energy if you can't help it. But show up. For Cassandra. For Luciana. For Samara." His voice softens. "For Katya. Let her see that her uncle is more than authority and intimidation. Let her see the man who loves fiercely enough to brand a witch to save his people, and who loves fiercely enough to seek forgiveness when he realizes the cost."

I look down at the wrapped grimoire. At the gift I'm bringing to a woman I wronged. To a party celebrating a holiday in the wrong season because one witch refused to let trauma win.

Vlad's right. Showing up is all any of us can do.

I stand, ready to grab my jacket—

But Vlad hasn't left.

He's still in the doorway, weight shifted to one foot, arms crossed. That easy confidence from earlier has dimmed into something heavier. More uncertain.

"There's something else," I say. Not a question. I've known Vlad long enough to read his tells.

Relief flashes across his face. "Yes."

He slips back into the chair across from my desk, and the way he settles—leaning forward, elbows on his knees—tells me this isn't casual. This is important.

"It's about Samara," he says.

My spine stiffens. "What about her?"

"Her relationship with Nikolaas Draken." He doesn't soften it, doesn't ease into the topic. "It needs to end."

"That's not your decision to make."

"No. It's yours." Vlad's voice is flat, certain.

I'm silent, processing this.

"You've seen them together," Vlad continues. "Tell me what you see."

I think about it. Really think about it, instead of just accepting the surface level of "Samara is happy, Samara is in love, Samara has made her choice."

What do I actually see?

"She's worn down," I admit slowly. "Thinner than she should be. Quieter."

"Exhausted," Vlad says. "Every time I've visited Paris these past months, she looks worse. More drained. And Nikolaas?" His expression darkens. "His dragon is volatile. Unstable. The curse is getting stronger, not weaker, and he's taking it out on everyone around him—especially her."

"They're trying to break the curse—"

"Are they?" Vlad interrupts. "Or is *she* trying while he spirals? Because from where I'm standing, she's carrying the entire weight of that relationship while he burns hotter and more dangerous every week."

The words land like blows because they're true.

I've been so consumed with Luciana's return—with the miracle of having her back, with adjusting to this new reality where the woman I love is alive again—that I've barely paid attention to my sister.

To the way she moves through the manor like a ghost.

To how she flinches when Nikolaas' eyes flash gold.

To the careful way she speaks around him, as if measuring every word for potential detonation.

"She loves him," I say, but even I can hear how weak it sounds.

"She's twenty years old," Vlad counters. "Too young by witch standards to be bonded. Too young to tie herself to a dragon who might burn her alive—literally or figuratively—before the year is out." He pauses. "And even when she turns twenty-one, you have the right as Ursa King to refuse the match. To refuse Nikolaas Draken's claim on her."

"She'd hate me for it."

"She might." Vlad doesn't flinch from the truth. "But she'd be alive. And free. And able to find someone who doesn't make her feel like she's walking on a knife's edge every moment they're together."

I stand, pace to the window. The Paris afternoon is fading into evening, spring flowers blooming in the private garden below.

"I can't make that decision for her," I say finally. "She's not a child anymore."

"No. But she's still your sister. Still your responsibility as Head of House." Vlad joins me at the window, his reflection meeting mine in the glass. "I'm not saying break them up tomorrow. I'm saying keep a close eye on her. *See* what's actually happening. And if it's as bad as I think it is—if Nikolaas' dragon is deteriorating and taking her down with him—then yes. Use your authority. End it before she's bound to him forever."

I can't argue with any of it.

"You think I've been neglecting her."

"I think you've been drunk on having Luciana back." Vlad's voice is gentle now, understanding. "And I don't blame you for that. You grieved for a year. You branded a witch and nearly destroyed yourself in the process. Now Luciana is here, and all you can see is her. I get it, brother. I do."

He turns to face me fully.

"But Samara is still here, too. Still living under your roof. Still trying to save a man who might not be savable. And she needs you to see that. To protect her, even if it's from herself."

I think about Cassandra's party tomorrow night. About Nikolaas and Samara arriving together. About the tension that radiates from him like heat, the way his dragon sits barely restrained beneath his skin.

About Kaisner, who will also be there. The dragon shifter who's been making moves, challenging Niko-laas' claim to the Draken throne.

"Tomorrow night could be a disaster," I say quietly.

"Tomorrow night will *absolutely* be a disaster," Vlad corrects. "Two dragons who hate each other in one room? While one of them is losing control, and the other is looking for any excuse to strike? It's going to go badly." He grips my shoulder. "Which is why you need to be ready. Watch Samara. Watch how she is with Nikolaas. And after the party, make your decision."

"And if she fights me on it?"

"Then you fight back." His grip tightens. "Because you're not just her brother, Gavriil. You're the Ursa King. And sometimes being king means making the choices others can't make for themselves."

He releases me, heads for the door again. This time, I know he's really leaving.

"One more thing," he says from the threshold. "If you do decide to end it—to refuse Nikolaas' claim— you need to be prepared for the fallout. The Drakens are a powerful family. Nikolaas won't accept it quietly. And Samara..." He trails off. "She'll see it as a betrayal. At first."

"But she'll forgive me eventually?"

"Maybe." Vlad's smile is sad. "Or maybe she'll hate you forever. But at least she'll be alive and whole to do it."

With that, he's gone.

I stand alone in my study, staring at the wrapped grimoire for Cassandra. At the gift meant to acknowledge her struggle, her power, her right to choose her own path.

And I think about Samara.

About choice versus protection.

About when a brother—a king—has the right to override someone's will for their own good.

About how I branded Cassandra for similar

reasons. For the greater good. For survival. And how much it cost her.

Can I really do that again? To my own sister?

Can I afford not to, if Vlad is right about Nikolaas?

Tomorrow night at the party, I'll watch.

And then I'll decide.

Even if the decision destroys whatever fragile relationship Samara and I have left.

6

JULIETTE: CHRISTMAS PAST

I'm standing in the Deveraux Manor dining room, alone with a glass of wine and the ghost of three hundred years, when the world fractures.

It starts with the scent. Not the pine and cinnamon of Cassandra's decorations waiting in boxes, but something older. Roasted goose. Mulled wine sweetened with honey. Beeswax candles burning in silver candelabras that haven't graced this table in centuries.

My hand trembles. The wine glass slips from my fingers.

It doesn't shatter.

Because I'm no longer standing. I'm sitting. And the glass in my hand is different—heavier crystal, filled with deep red burgundy instead of modern cabernet. My gown has changed too. I look down to find myself in emerald silk, the kind I haven't worn since—

"Maman! Maman, look!"

My heart stops.

Charlotte.

She's three years old, her copper curls escaping the ribbon I tied this morning—*this morning? No, three hundred years ago*—her green eyes bright with mischief as she holds up a wooden horse. One of Henri's birthday gifts, though she's claimed it as her own.

"That's Henri's, *ma petite*," I hear myself say, my voice younger, lighter. Unscarred by centuries of grief.

"But he's only *one*," Charlotte protests with the iron logic of a three-year-old. "He doesn't know how to play properly yet."

"Charlotte Deveraux." I try to sound stern, but my lips curve into a smile I can't control. "Return your brother's gift this instant."

She pouts, lower lip trembling in that way she perfected at age two. But before she can deploy the full force of her charm, young Willem swoops in—my wild five-year-old son with his father's golden hair and boundless energy.

"I'll trade you," he announces, offering a wooden sword. "This is much better for fighting dragons."

"But you *are* a dragon," Charlotte says, confused.

"Exactly!" young Willem grins, showing the gap where he lost his first tooth last month. "That's why I need to practice fighting *other* dragons. For when I'm grown and Papa lets me shift."

"Willem, darling, eat your pudding," I say, watching him abandon the sword to chase his twin sisters around the table. Elisabeth and Margaretha—eight years old, identical save for the fact that Elisabeth's magic already crackles visibly in her fingertips while Margaretha's manifests more subtly, in the way frost patterns bloom on her water glass.

"Girls, no magic at the table," I call out, but my tone is indulgent. It's Christmas. It's Henri's first birthday. I can feel the joy bubbling in my chest, effervescent as champagne.

At the head of the table, Jan—my serious ten-year-old with his father's ice-blue eyes and my stubborn chin—is explaining something to Colette. My eldest daughter, twelve and already showing signs of the powerful witch she'll become, listens with the patience of someone far older than her years.

"And then the dragon swooped down—" Jan gestures wildly, nearly knocking over his goblet.

"Careful, *mon chou*," I say, steadying it with a flick of magic.

"Sorry, Maman." But he's grinning, unrepentant, and continues his tale.

At the far end of the table, in his wooden high chair, Henri sits like a tiny king. One year old today. My youngest—my last, I know somehow, though I haven't told Willem yet. The baby's blonde hair curls at his temples, sticky with cake. His blue eyes—so like his father's—track the chaos of his siblings with solemn fascination.

"Alright, *mes enfants*," Colette announces, rising with the authority of the eldest. "Time for nursery. Nanny is waiting."

A chorus of protests rises, predictable as sunrise.

"But it's Henri's birthday!"

"We haven't finished playing!"

"I don't want to go to bed!"

"Charlotte needs her rest," I say gently, catching my youngest daughter as she attempts to hide under the table. "And Henri is already falling asleep in his pudding."

It's true. The baby's eyes are drooping, his little fist curled around a silver spoon he's too young to properly use.

Colette moves with efficiency, gathering Charlotte despite her squirming protests. Jan scoops up Henri with surprising gentleness for a ten-year-old boy, supporting the baby's head the way I taught him. The twins file out hand-in-hand, still arguing about whether ice magic or fire magic is superior for Christmas celebrations.

"Go with Nanny," I tell young Willem, who's making one last heroic stand by the pudding bowl. "If you're very good, perhaps Papa will show you dragon scales tomorrow."

The boy's eyes light up. "Promise?"

From the shadows near the hearth, Willem speaks for the first time this evening. "I promise, little dragon."

His voice.

Gods, his voice. I'd forgotten how it sounded before the darkness crept in. Warm as summer fire, with that slight roughness that always made my pulse quicken. Young. Unburdened.

This is the Willem I loved.

Young Willem races out after his siblings, leaving a trail of excited shouting about dragon scales and Christmas miracles. Colette pauses at the door, my responsible eldest, already more woman than child.

"Goodnight, Maman. Goodnight, Papa."

"Bonne nuit, *ma chérie*," I whisper.

Then she's gone too, and we're alone.

The dining room settles into stillness. Candles flicker in their silver holders, casting dancing shadows across the remains of our feast. The fire crackles in the hearth. Outside, snow falls soft and silent against ancient windowpanes.

Willem rises from his chair with the fluid grace of a predator. Or a king. He's both now—the Dragon King, recently proclaimed, authority recognized across every supernatural territory in Europe.

He's thirty-two years old in this moment, at the absolute peak of his power. The dragon and the man are still in perfect balance—the beast's strength tempered by the man's heart. His golden hair catches the candlelight as he moves toward me, and he's magnificent in the way only a dragon king can be— dangerous and perfect and utterly magnetic.

"Finally," he says, voice dropping to that low rumble that always shoots a thrill through my being. "Peace and quiet."

I laugh softly. "You say that as if you don't love the chaos."

"I love the chaos." He reaches me, one hand settling possessively at my waist. "But I *also* love the moments after. When the house settles. When the children are asleep. When I finally have you to myself again."

His thumb traces slow circles against the silk of my gown, and heat pools low in my belly despite spending the entire day managing seven children.

"We had a moment of peace this morning," I remind him, trying to sound prim even as I lean into his touch.

"That was twelve hours ago." His other hand comes up to cup my face, tilting it toward his. "I've been watching you all evening, *ma reine.* Watching you with our children. Being magnificent and patient and so beautiful, it hurts to look at you. Do you have any idea what you do to me?"

"Willem—" I start, but he's already pulling me closer.

"Dance with me," he says, and it's not a request.

I blink.

"There's no music."

"Does that matter?" He offers his hand, and even knowing what I know—what he'll become, what we'll lose—I cannot refuse.

My palm slides into his. The touch sends warmth racing up my arm, familiar and devastating. He pulls me to my feet, one hand settling at my waist, the other cradling my fingers as if I'm made of spun glass.

We begin to move.

There is no music. Just the whisper of silk against wool, the soft shuffle of our feet across the floor, the crackle of the fire. But Willem hums—low and tuneless, more feeling than melody—and I rest my head against his chest and let him lead me in slow circles around the table where our seven children just feasted.

Seven children.

The thought pierces me with sudden, vicious clarity. Seven children I carried, birthed, nursed. Seven souls I loved more than magic, more than power, more than my own life.

All of them gone. Dead. Dust for centuries.

"You're thinking too much," Willem murmurs against my hair. His breath is warm, scented with wine and cinnamon. "I can feel your mind racing."

"I'm thinking about how perfect this is," I lie. Or perhaps it's not a lie. Perhaps both things can be true.

"Perfect," he echoes, and spins me gently beneath his arm. When I return to him, his ice-blue eyes are serious. "Do you know what I see when I look at you?"

"A tired mother covered in cake?" I try to laugh, but my voice catches.

"I see my queen." His hand tightens on my waist. "My equal. The woman who gave me seven miracles and still manages to be the most powerful witch in Europe. The woman who chose me despite every reason not to."

Oh, Willem. If you only knew.

If you only knew that I chose you because I had no choice. That your dragon claimed me before I was old enough to understand what claiming meant. That I learned to love you the way a bird learns to love its cage—by making beauty of captivity.

But that's not entirely fair, is it?

Because in this moment—in this perfect Christmas evening with our children sleeping safely upstairs and his arms around me and the world reduced to candlelight and warmth—I do love him. Completely. Desperately.

Before the possessiveness. Before the darkness. Before the dragon consumed the man.

"I will love you forever," Willem says, and his voice cracks with emotion. Dragon fire dances in his eyes, pure gold unmarred by the corruption that will eventually claim him. "Through every lifetime. Every incarnation. Even if you forget me, even if you choose another, my soul will always recognize yours."

The words are a vow. A promise.

A curse.

"Willem—" I start to say, but then the world *shifts*.

The candlelight flickers. Dims. I see double for a moment—Willem young and beautiful before me, but also Willem as he became. Eyes gone cold. Magic turned to frost. The dragon wearing his skin but no longer tempered by the man's heart.

"No," I whisper. "Not yet. Please, not yet."

But time is fracturing. I can feel it in the way the floorboards beneath my feet turn from warm wood to cold marble. In the way Willem's hand becomes incorporeal, his fingers passing through mine like smoke.

"Juliette?" His voice is fading. "What's wrong?"

Everything. Everything is wrong.

The dining room blurs. Our seven children's chairs become empty. The feast becomes dust. The candles gutter and die, replaced by modern electric lights that won't exist for another two hundred years.

"I'm sorry," I choke out, though I don't know if I'm apologizing to Willem or to our children or to myself. "I'm so sorry for all of it."

"For what?" Willem reaches for me, but his hand passes through my shoulder. He's becoming transparent, a ghost of a memory of a ghost. "Juliette, I don't understand—"

"I know," I sob. "You don't. You can't. You won't understand until it's too late, until the dragon eats your heart, until you become something I can't love, can't save, can't—"

Reality snaps.

I'm alone.

The dining room is empty save for boxes of Christmas decorations waiting to be hung. My wine glass lies shattered on the floor—when did I drop it?— red liquid spreading across marble like blood.

I'm wearing jeans and a cashmere sweater, not emerald silk. My hair is shorter, styled in a modern cut. Three hundred years separate me from the woman who danced with Willem while their children slept.

The children.

Oh gods, the children.

I press my hands to my mouth, but I can't stop the sound that escapes—half sob, half keen, the grief of centuries compressed into a single moment of loss.

"Juliette?"

Ivan's voice. Present. Real. *Now.*

I spin to find him in the doorway, his green eyes wide with concern. He's holding a box labeled "ORNA-MENTS" in Cassandra's aggressive scrawl, but he sets it down immediately when he sees my face.

"What happened?" He's beside me in an instant, hands on my shoulders, solid and warm and *here*. "Are you hurt?"

"No. Yes. I don't—" I can't form coherent words. "I saw them. I saw all of them."

"Saw who?" His thumb brushes my cheek, and I realize I'm crying.

"My children." The words break on a sob. "Willem. Christmas. Henri's first birthday. They were here, Ivan. Right here in this room. And then they were gone. They're always gone."

Understanding dawns in his eyes. "A temporal clash."

"Cassandra's magic," I manage, trying to steady myself. "Her pregnancy is creating warps. I've seen Willem three times now. But this time it wasn't just him. It was all of them. My babies. My—" I break off, pressing my fist to my mouth.

Seven children I loved. Seven children who lived and died and turned to dust while I remained—not truly immortal, but suspended. Trapped in a waiting room of my own making, a spell-crafted liminal space where I existed between death and life, holding onto memory while I searched for a body to inhabit. Jeanette's body, when it finally came. But the price of that spell was remembering everything. Every moment. Every loss. Every face of every child I could never hold again.

Ivan pulls me into his arms. I resist for half a heartbeat—some distant part of me still standing in 1687, still feeling Willem's hands at my waist—but then I collapse into him. Let him hold me while I shake apart.

"I'm sorry," he murmurs into my hair. "I'm so sorry, *mon cœur.*"

"They were so young," I whisper. "Charlotte was three. Henri had just turned one. Willem was dancing with me, and there was no music, just us, just—" My voice breaks. "It was perfect. And I knew it was all going to end. I knew what Willem would become. What I'd lose. But for those few moments, I got to have them back."

Ivan's arms tighten. "That's why you understand."

"Understand what?"

"Why Cassandra needs this party." He pulls back just enough to look at me. "Why she's throwing Christmas in May. Why she's gathering everyone despite knowing it could end in disaster."

I blink at him through tears. "Because she's making new memories to replace the ones that haunt her."

"Exactly." His hand cups my face with infinite gentleness. "Last Christmas was torture for her. Alone. Branded. Afraid. So she's taking it back. Claiming joy from darkness. Making her own Christmas on her own terms."

I look around the dining room. In my mind's eye, I can still see the feast from 1687. Seven children laughing. Willem young and beautiful. Love before it curdled into possession.

But I can also see what this room will become in a few hours. Cassandra's chosen family gathered around this same table. Vampires and witches and shifters who've chosen each other despite centuries of enmity. Ivan beside me, offering the freedom Willem never could. Dristan protecting Cassandra with the fierce devotion I once craved. All of them alive, present, creating new joy from old pain.

"She reminds me of myself," I say quietly. "Young. Powerful. Determined to make beauty despite the darkness."

"You still do that," Ivan says. "Every day."

"Do I?" I touch the scattered ornaments on the floor. "Or am I just haunted by ghosts of Christmases past?"

"Both." He kneels to pick up pieces of broken glass. "You carry your grief, and you create new joy. They're not mutually exclusive."

I help him gather the shards, and as I do, I feel something settle in my chest. An understanding. An acceptance.

I loved Willem. I loved our children. That Christmas in 1687 was real and perfect and precious.

And it's gone.

But this—this chosen family, this Christmas in May, this chance to help Cassandra reclaim joy—this is real too. Different. Strange. Completely absurd.

And maybe that's the point.

"Tell me about them," Ivan says softly, settling beside me on the floor amid broken crystal and spilled wine. "Your children. I want to know."

So I do.

I tell him about Colette's quiet strength and Elisabeth's wild magic. About Jan's serious eyes and young Willem's dragon dreams. About Margaretha making it snow indoors and Charlotte's irresistible pouts. About Henri, my Christmas baby, who would grow up to be a healer before plague claimed him at sixty-one.

I tell him about the Christmas when they were all small enough to fit in my lap. When the world was simpler, and love hadn't yet learned to wound.

And Ivan listens. Doesn't interrupt. Doesn't try to fix anything. Just sits with me in the wreckage and lets me remember.

When I finally fall silent, he speaks quietly. "I've never fathered children."

I look at him, surprised by the admission.

"Not once," he continues, his green eyes distant. "Not in three hundred years. Dristan always said it was a mercy—that immortality is harsh enough without watching your children age and die while you remain unchanged." His hand tightens on mine. "I never understood what he meant. Not really. Not until now."

"It is harsh," I whisper. "The harshest thing I've ever endured. Harder than Willem's darkness. Harder than dying. Harder than the waiting room where I existed for centuries, holding onto their faces, their voices, every memory burning like live coals I couldn't set down."

"And yet you endured it." There's something akin to awe in his voice. "Seven times over. Seven children you loved knowing you'd outlive them all. That takes a strength I'm not sure I possess."

"It's not strength." I shake my head. "It's just... love. You don't choose to stop loving them just because you know it will hurt. You love them anyway. You love them *because* they're mortal, because their time is precious, because every Christmas morning and birthday and ordinary Tuesday is a gift you'll never get back."

Ivan's thumb brushes across my knuckles. "I admire you for it. For carrying all that love and all that loss and still being willing to love again. Still being willing to help Cassandra celebrate. Still choosing to be here instead of drowning in three centuries of grief."

"Some days I do drown," I admit. "Some days I wake up and remember Charlotte's laugh or Henri's first steps, and I can barely breathe. But then..." I look around the room, at the absurd decorations, at Ivan's patient face. "Then there's this. New family. New love. New chances to make joy even when the timing is completely wrong."

"Christmas in May," he says softly.

"Christmas in May," I agree. "Because we're still here. Still choosing each other. And that has to mean something."

He leans forward and kisses my forehead with such

gentleness that it makes my chest ache. "It means everything."

"Thank you," I whisper when my voice finally runs dry.

"For what?"

"For being here. For letting me grieve them without trying to replace them."

He takes my hand. "I could never replace them. I wouldn't want to."

"No." I squeeze his fingers. "But you give me something Willem never could."

"What's that?"

"Choice." The word comes out clear and certain. "You let me choose you every day. You don't bind or claim or possess. You just... stay. And let me decide if I want to stay too."

His eyes go soft. "That's all I've ever wanted to give you."

We sit there for a long moment, hands entwined, surrounded by the debris of both past and present. Outside, May sunshine streams through windows where snow once fell. Cassandra's laughter echoes from somewhere upstairs, followed by Dristan's patient murmur.

Life. Present. Real.

"We should help her," I say finally. "With the decorations. The party."

"Are you sure?" Ivan searches my face. "If the temporal warps are becoming stronger—"

"Then I'll face them." I stand, pulling him up with

me. "But I won't let the past steal the present. Not anymore."

He smiles. "That's my girl."

Together, we clean up the spilled wine and broken glass. Then we open boxes and pull out Cassandra's ridiculous May Christmas decorations—black roses wound with silver bells, gothic wreaths heavy with mistletoe, ornaments shaped like skulls wearing tiny Santa hats.

"She has… interesting taste," Ivan observes, holding up a particularly macabre piece.

"She's making it her own." I hang the skull on an imaginary tree. "Not following tradition. Not trying to recreate something she lost. Just… creating something new."

"Like you," he says quietly.

"Like all of us." I turn to him. "We've all lost something. Christmas, lovers, children, lives. But we're still here. Still choosing each other. Still making joy even when it's absurd."

"Even when it's May," he teases.

"*Especially* when it's May."

Ivan's arms come around me, and this embrace is nothing like Willem's. It's lighter. Freer. Unchained by dragon fire or magical brands or possessive love.

It's a choice we both make, every single day.

And as I rest my head against his shoulder in the dining room where I once danced with a dead husband while my dead children slept, I realize something:

I'm not haunted by the past.

I'm blessed by it.

Because loving and losing seven children taught me how precious family is. Loving and losing Willem taught me the difference between possession and devotion. Three hundred years of grief taught me that joy is worth fighting for, even when the timing is completely wrong.

"Help me hang the mistletoe," I tell Ivan. "Cassandra wants it everywhere."

"Of course she does." But he's smiling as he reaches for the box.

We work in comfortable silence, transforming the dining room into Cassandra's vision of Christmas in spring. And when we're done, I stand back and survey our work.

The room looks nothing like it did in 1687. Everything is different—the decorations, the furniture, the people.

But the love is the same.

The choice to gather. To celebrate. To make beauty from darkness and joy from grief.

"Perfect," I whisper.

"It's completely absurd," Ivan corrects.

"Yes." I smile. "That too."

And for the first time since the temporal warp dragged me into the past, I feel at peace with both what I've lost and what I've found.

Christmas in May.

Why not?

After all, love isn't about perfect timing.

It's about being willing.

Willing to show up. Willing to choose each other. Willing to dance even when there's no music.

Just like Willem and I did, three hundred years ago, while our children slept.

Just like Ivan and I will do tonight, while Cassandra's chosen family gathers to reclaim joy from darkness.

The past and the present, meeting in mistletoe and memories.

Both precious.

Both real.

Both mine.

7

IVAN: THE ART OF GIVING

There's a Christmas tree in Deveraux Manor.

In May.

I've lived three hundred years. Survived the plague, the French Revolution, two World Wars, and Alisa's particularly vindictive brand of emotional terrorism. But somehow, a twelve-foot Norwegian spruce decorated with black roses and skull-shaped baubles in the middle of spring might finally break me.

"It's festive," Juliette said this morning, when she caught me glaring at it.

"It's ridiculous," I replied.

"You're helping anyway."

"Obviously." Because I'm a fool in love, and Juliette's smile is worth tolerating Cassandra's gleeful disregard for calendars and common sense.

Which is how I find myself on the Champs-Élysées at twilight, the last rays of sunset painting Paris in shades of gold and rose, walking beside Dristan and contemplating the particular circle of hell reserved for Secret Santa participants.

"You could just give him a bottle of vodka," Dristan suggests, hands in the pockets of his perfectly tailored charcoal suit. Even after a thousand years, my maker manages to look like he stepped out of a Renaissance painting—all sharp cheekbones and brooding intensity. "Russians appreciate vodka."

"Gavriil Alexeev is the Ursa King," I say flatly. "Alpha of the Russian shifter community with authority recognized worldwide. I can't give him a bottle of Stolichnaya like he's some uncle at a family reunion."

"Why not?"

"Because he'll think I'm being dismissive."

"You *are* being dismissive."

"Yes, but I can't let him *know* that." I pause in front of a tech shop, peering through the window at the latest gadgets. "It has to be thoughtful enough that Cassandra doesn't kill me, expensive enough that Gavriil can't complain, but impersonal enough that I'm not suggesting we're actually friends."

Dristan's lips quirk into something almost resembling a smile. "The delicate art of hostile gift-giving."

"Exactly." I adjust my sunglasses—Persol, because immortality is no excuse for poor taste. "Besides, Samara mentioned he's obsessed with technology. The man has a smart home system that probably achieves sentience during full moons."

"How very modern of him."

"He livestreams his pack meetings, Dristan. *Livestreams*. Like some sort of furry tech bro."

My maker actually laughs at that—a rare sound that makes passing mortals turn and stare. Dristan has that effect on people. Three centuries of knowing him, and I'm still not immune.

"You're enjoying this," I accuse.

"Immensely." He starts walking again, that unhurried vampire grace that makes everyone else look clumsy by comparison. "It's nice to see you stressed about something other than Juliette's safety for once."

"I'm always stressed about Juliette's safety."

"I know. It's exhausting to witness." He pauses, then adds with suspicious casualness, "How are you handling it?"

"Handling what?"

"The baby."

I nearly trip over my feet. A mortal couple walking a small dog gives me an odd look. I ignore them.

"Cassandra's baby has nothing to do with me," I say carefully.

"Doesn't it?" Dristan stops in front of a luxury electronics boutique. "Your girlfriend's great-great-great-however-many-greats granddaughter is pregnant. A new generation of Deveraux. You'll be an unofficial uncle."

"I prefer 'sarcastic family friend.'"

"Sibling rivalry, then." His dark eyes gleam with amusement. "I wonder if you'll enter the *terrible twos* phase. Start acting out for attention. Refusing to share your toys."

"I'm three hundred years old."

"Emotionally, you're about twelve."

"Says the vampire who broods in his palazzo like a gothic romance novel protagonist."

"I don't brood. I *contemplate*."

"You brood."

We're both smiling now, that easy rapport we're building. People think being turned by someone creates this mystical bond of maker and fledgling, all dramatic and intense. Sometimes it does. But mostly, it's like this—two immortals who've known each other long enough to weaponize affection.

"In all seriousness," Dristan says, his tone shifting to something gentler. "How are you? With everything changing. Cassandra pregnant. Juliette settling into modern life. Your entire found family evolving."

I consider the question.

"Terrified," I admit. "Grateful. Occasionally, homicidal toward anyone who might threaten them. The usual."

"The usual," he echoes. "Ivan, you're allowed to want things. To be part of this new chapter they're building."

"I know."

"Do you?" He turns to face me fully. "Because for three hundred years, you've been the one standing at the edges. Observing. Protecting from a distance.

Making sure everyone else gets their happy ending while you—"

"While I get Juliette back from the dead and get to love her without the shadow of Willem's dragon breathing down my neck?" I interrupt. "I'd say I'm doing fairly well, Dad."

I use the term deliberately—*Dad*—drawing it out with just enough mockery to make him grimace. He hates it when I call him that.

"I'm your maker, not your father."

"Vampire dad, then."

"Absolutely not."

"Sire? Progenitor? Papa Dristan?"

"Ivan."

"Fine." I grin at his discomfort. "But you started it with the sibling rivalry nonsense."

He shakes his head, but there's warmth in his expression. "Come. Let's find something for the Ursa King before you spiral into an existential crisis about your place in the family dynamic."

"Too late."

We enter the boutique, all sleek glass and minimalist design. A sales associate materializes immediately—young, sharply dressed, with that particular Parisian combination of helpfulness and judgment.

"*Bonjour, messieurs.* How may I assist you?"

"I need a gift," I say. "For someone who has everything, wants nothing I'd willingly give him, and will probably hate me regardless of what I choose."

The associate blinks. "Ah. A... difficult recipient."

"The Ursa King," Dristan supplies helpfully.

"I'm sorry?"

"Never mind." I wave a dismissive hand. "He's a tech enthusiast. Russian. Likes to feel powerful and in control. What do you have that screams 'I respect you enough to spend money on you but not enough to actually care what you think'?"

The associate looks between us, clearly trying to determine if we're serious.

"Perhaps... a smartwatch?" he offers tentatively.

"Too personal."

"Wireless headphones?"

"Too common."

"A drone?"

I pause. "Does it have a camera?"

"Of course."

"Perfect for spying on one's enemies," Dristan murmurs.

"Or wildlife," the associate adds quickly. "Photography. Surveillance of... nature."

I'm about to respond when a familiar voice cuts through the boutique's ambient electronica.

"Ivan Lockhart. Shopping for technology. The apocalypse must be imminent."

I turn to find Samara Alexeeva standing near the tablet display, looking remarkably unbearlike in a flowing cream dress and leather jacket. Beside her, Clarissa—Nikolaas' younger sister—examines a smart home device with the intensity of someone reading ancient prophecy.

"Samara." I nod to her, then to Clarissa. "I didn't realize witches and dragon shifters required electronics to function."

"We don't," Samara says, crossing to us with that peculiar grace all Ursa have—fluid and dangerous and somehow gentle. "But Clarissa is convinced that if she programs her coffee maker correctly, she can predict the future through the patterns of the foam."

"It's not *that* absurd," Clarissa protests, not looking up from the device. "Scrying through technology is a perfectly valid modern adaptation of ancient practices."

"She's been trying to hack her espresso machine for two weeks," Samara adds.

"And I'm getting close."

Dristan looks genuinely intrigued. "Can you actually do that?"

"Theoretically." Clarissa finally glances up, her pale blue eyes distant. "Though the visions are mostly about needing to descale the machine. Very mundane prophecies."

Despite myself, I laugh. "Cassandra would love that. Apocalyptic visions delivered via latte art."

"Speaking of Cassandra," Samara says, her dark eyes sharp. "I hear you drew my brother for Secret Santa."

"Your sources are alarmingly accurate."

"Cassandra told me." She smirks. "She thinks it's hilarious. As do I."

"I'm delighted to provide entertainment."

"What are you planning to get him?" She moves closer, examining me with the assessing gaze of someone who knows Gavriil intimately. "It can't be too expensive, or he'll think you're trying to show him up. Can't be too cheap or he'll think you're insulting him. Can't be too personal or he'll be uncomfortable. Can't be too impersonal or—"

"Yes, thank you, I'm aware of the impossible parameters." I run a hand through my hair. "Hence the shopping trip with Dristan. Who, despite being a thousand years old, has been spectacularly unhelpful."

"I suggested vodka."

"You suggested *Stolichnaya*."

"What's wrong with Stolichnaya?"

"Everything," Samara and I say in unison.

Clarissa drifts over, still holding the smart home device. "Gavriil likes things that make him feel in control. Things he can monitor, adjust, optimize. His entire manor runs on automated systems."

"See?" I gesture to her. "This is helpful."

"Get him something for his smart home," Clarissa continues, her prophet's gaze going slightly unfocused. "Something... unique. High-end. But also..." She pauses. "You should add something ridiculous to it. Something that will make him laugh despite himself."

"Gavriil doesn't laugh."

"He does," Samara corrects. "Just rarely. And usually at other people's expense." She considers. "Clarissa's right, though. Get him tech, but make it personal. Show him you actually thought about it."

I look at Dristan. "Did you plan this ambush?"

"I'm as surprised as you are."

"Liar."

Samara starts browsing the displays with the focused intensity of a bear on a hunt. Within minutes, she's found something—a sleek smart home hub with built-in AI, voice control, and enough features to make even my tech-savvy heart beat faster.

"This," she declares. "It's new. Expensive. Integrates with everything he already has. And the AI can be programmed with custom responses."

"Custom responses?"

"You can make it say whatever you want." Her grin is absolutely wicked. "Imagine Gavriil asking his house to turn on the lights, and it responds in, say... a Russian accent. Or Luciana's voice. Or—"

"My voice," I finish, suddenly seeing the brilliance. "Saying appropriately sarcastic things every time he gives a command."

"Exactly."

"That's perfect." I turn to the hovering sales associate. "I'll take it."

"Excellent choice, *monsieur*."

As he rings up the purchase—eye-wateringly expensive, but worth it for the chaos potential—Clarissa speaks quietly beside me.

"You're worried about the party."

It's not a question. Seers never ask questions.

"Should I be?"

"Things will spiral," she says calmly. "Magic will clash. Tempers will flare. Someone will probably cry. Possibly someone will bleed." She pauses. "But in the end, it will matter. The gathering. The attempt. The choosing to celebrate despite knowing it might end badly."

I stare at her, positively disappointed.

"That's... remarkably unhelpful."

"I'm a seer, not a reassurer."

Samara rejoins us, holding a small additional item—a USB drive shaped like a bear.

"Add this," she says. "Pre-program it with something obnoxious. Gavriil will hate it and love it simultaneously."

I take the ridiculous contraption, hold it up to eye level.

"Your brother is very confusing."

"He's a Ursa King who brands witches against their will and then develops a conscience," Samara replies offhandedly. "Confusion is his natural state."

Fair point.

We complete the purchase—the smart home hub, the bear USB, and a very expensive gift box that makes everything look more elegant than it has any right to be.

Outside, dusk has settled over Paris, the air cooling as evening approaches. Dristan checks his phone—probably Cassandra summoning him for some party-related emergency.

"I should go," he says. "She wants help moving furniture."

"At six months pregnant?"

"She's *levitating* the furniture. I'm there to make sure she doesn't accidentally launch it through a window."

"I see. Moral support for domestic destruction."

He clasps my shoulder briefly—his version of affection. "You did well, Ivan. With the gift. With... everything."

"Ah. High praise from Papa Dristan."

He scowls. "Don't."

I grin as he walks away, shaking his head.

Samara and Clarissa remain, the two of them looking at me with matching expressions of amusement.

"So," Samara says. "Are you going to program the AI, or should I?"

"Oh, I'm absolutely doing it myself." I hold up the USB bear. "This requires a delicate touch. A perfect balance of respect and mockery."

"You're going to make it insult him, aren't you."

"Only mildly."

Clarissa's eyes go distant again. "He'll threaten to throw it out a window. Then keep it forever."

"Perfect."

We part ways—Samara and Clarissa back to their coffee machine prophecy project, me toward home with my perfectly passive-aggressive gift.

As I walk, I program the AI on my phone, loading the custom responses onto the bear drive:

"Good evening, your majesty. The lights are on. Try not to trip over your own ego."

"Temperature adjusted. Unlike your emotional availability."

"Security system armed. Though we both know nothing is more dangerous than Luciana when you've annoyed her."

Petty? Absolutely.

Hilarious? Undoubtedly.

This will be the gift that keeps on giving.

Will Gavriil actually appreciate it beneath the layers of Ursa King dignity?

Clarissa says yes.

And seers are rarely wrong.

By the time I reach Deveraux Manor, I'm actually looking forward to the party. Not for the Christmas-in-May absurdity. Not for the inevitable magical disasters Clarissa predicted.

But for the moment when Gavriil opens this gift, realizes what I've done, and has to decide whether to kill me or laugh.

Worth it either way.

I find Juliette in the kitchen, sampling Dristan's latest batch of cookies—somehow perfect this time.

"Did you find something?" she asks.

"I found chaos." I show her the box. "Wrapped in expensive electronics and bear-shaped spite."

She laughs, and the sound fills the kitchen with warmth that has nothing to do with the oven.

"You're terrible."

"I prefer 'creatively hostile.'"

"That too." She kisses me, tasting of sugar and cinnamon. "Cassandra will love it."

"Gavriil will hate it."

"Even better."

And there, in the kitchen of Deveraux Manor, with my love in my arms and a spite-gift in a box and a Christmas tree in May waiting in the great hall, it dawns on me.

This. This is family.

Ridiculous. Chaotic. Absolutely perfect.

Exactly as it should be.

8

SAM: FIRE AND SECRETS

'm standing in front of my bedroom mirror, trying to decide between the black dress and the crimson one, when my door creaks open.

My skin prickles with warmth, the air around me heating like standing near an open furnace.

A thrill rushes through my veins when his reflection appears behind mine.

Golden blonde hair, ice-blue eyes that catch the afternoon light. He doesn't say anything. Just stands there, filling the doorway, radiating that controlled tension he wears like armor.

Nik shouldn't be here. The party doesn't start for two hours, and worse, *Gavriil is home*. My brother, the Ursa King, who would lose his mind if he knew Nikolaas Draken was in my bedroom.

He's downstairs in his study with Luciana. I can hear the low rumble of his voice, the soft sound of her laughter. Based on the utterly besotted look on his face this morning, he's not paying attention to anything except her. But that doesn't mean he couldn't walk upstairs at any moment.

Which means Nikolaas knows *exactly* how dangerous this is.

And he's doing it anyway.

The knock on my door is barely a courtesy. He's already stepping inside, already filling my space with heat and want and that particular tension that's been building between us for months.

"Nik—" I start, but the words die when I see his eyes.

Gold. Pure molten gold with barely a ring of ice-blue remaining.

His dragon is right there. Right at the surface. Closer than I've ever seen it outside of a shift.

"You can't be here," I manage, even as my body betrays me, heating under his gaze. "Gavriil is downstairs—"

"With Luciana." Nikolaas closes the door behind him. Locks it. The soft click echoes like a gunshot. "Heard them laughing in his study on my way up."

"Exactly. He could come up any second—"

"I don't care." He crosses the room in three strides. Dragon-fast. Predator-fast. "I need you, Samara. Right now. I can't walk into that party tonight without having you first."

His hands cup my face, and his skin is burning. Not metaphorically. Literally hot, the way it gets when his dragon is too close to the surface.

"Your eyes," I whisper.

"I know." His thumb traces my lower lip, and the touch sends heat spiraling through my core. "He's been like this all day. Restless. Demanding. He wants—" He stops, jaw clenching.

"Wants what?"

"You." The word comes out rough. Raw. "To claim you. Brand you. Make you his in every way that matters."

My breath catches. We've danced around this for months. The wanting. The waiting. The fact that I'm still too young by witch standards, that we can't make it official until my twenty-first birthday.

Twenty days away.

Twenty days that feel like an eternity when he's looking at me like this.

"We can't," I say, but my hands are already fisting in his shirt, pulling him closer. "Not yet. You know we can't."

"Can't brand you." His forehead drops to mine, and I can feel him shaking with the effort of control. "Can't claim you the way my dragon demands. But I can have you, Samara. Here. Now. I need to have you, or I'm going to lose my fucking mind before we even get to that goddamn party."

"Gavriil is right downstairs—"

"I know." His hands slide down to my waist, gripping hard enough to bruise. "And I don't care. Let him try to stop me. Let him try to keep me from what's mine."

"I'm not yours yet," I remind him, even as my body melts into his touch. "Not officially."

"Technicality." His mouth crashes onto mine, and I taste smoke and need and desperation. "You've been mine since the moment we met. The rest is just paperwork. Juliette was eighteen when Willem branded her. Eighteen. You're twenty years and eleven months old. Close enough."

"Not by witch law—"

"Fuck witch law." His hands are sliding under my robe, finding bare skin. "Twenty days, Sam. Twenty more days of this torture. But right now, I need you."

I should push him away. Should remind him that we're in my brother's house, that this is reckless, that if Gavriil catches us—

But then Nikolaas' hands are cupping my breasts through the thin silk, and I stop thinking entirely.

"Bed," he growls against my mouth. "Now."

It's not a request.

I let him walk me backward until my legs hit the mattress. He doesn't push me down—not yet. Instead, he pulls back just enough to look at me, and the gold in his eyes is luminous, mesmerizing.

"Tell me to stop," he says, voice strained. "If you don't want this. If it's too much. Tell me now, because once I start, I'm not going to be gentle."

My heart pounds. We've been together before. Made love in his rooms at Draken Manor, careful and quiet and always with one ear listening for interruptions. But this feels different. Sharper. More dangerous.

"I don't want you to be gentle," I whisper.

Something in him breaks.

He kisses me again, harder this time, his tongue claiming my mouth with the same possessive intensity his dragon wants to claim all of me. His hands make quick work of my robe, sliding it off my shoulders until it puddles at my feet.

I'm wearing nothing underneath.

"Fuck." The word is half prayer, half curse. "You're going to kill me."

"That's the idea."

His laugh is dark and rough. Then his hands are on me—everywhere. Cupping my breasts, thumbs circling my nipples until I gasp. Sliding down my ribs, my hips, gripping my ass hard enough that I know I'll have fingerprint bruises tomorrow.

Good.

I want to be marked by him, even if it can't be official yet.

"Bed," he says again, and this time he does push me down.

I land on my back, and before I can catch my breath, he's on me. Covering me. His weight pressing me into the mattress as his mouth finds my throat.

"Twenty days," he murmurs against my pulse. "Twenty days until I can do this properly. Brand you. Make you my queen."

"Queen?" I manage, even as his teeth scrape my neck.

"My queen." His hand slides between my thighs, finding me wet and ready. "When I take the Dragon King title from Kaisner—and I will—you'll rule beside me. My equal. My mate. Mine."

He slides a finger inside me, and I arch off the bed with a strangled moan.

"Shh." His free hand covers my mouth. "Quiet, Little Bear. Unless you want your brother to hear what I'm doing to you."

The reminder that we could be caught—that Gavriil is literally downstairs and could walk up at any moment—sends a thrill of fear and arousal through me. My brother could open that door. Could find Nikolaas in my bed, his hands on me, claiming what isn't officially his yet.

The danger makes it hotter.

Nikolaas seems to sense my thoughts because his smile turns wicked. He adds another finger, working me with devastating intention while his thumb finds my most sensitive spot.

"You like that," he murmurs. "The risk. Knowing we could get caught."

I nod against his palm, unable to form words.

"Good girl." The praise makes me clench around his fingers. "Because I'm going to make you come so hard you forget your own name. And you're going to be quiet about it. Understand?"

I nod again.

He removes his hand from my mouth, replacing it with his lips as his fingers work faster. His kiss swallows my moans as pleasure builds, coiling tighter and tighter in my core.

"That's it," he breathes against my mouth. "Come for me, Sam. Show me you're mine."

I shatter. Release rips through me like dragon fire, and I barely manage to muffle my cry against his shoulder. He works me through it, drawing out every last tremor until I'm boneless and gasping.

"Beautiful," he murmurs, withdrawing his hand. "But we're not done."

He stands long enough to strip off his shirt, and I drink in the sight of him.

His body is carved muscle and heat. Dragon scales shimmer beneath his skin—gold and bronze, visible for just a moment before sinking back below the surface. The dragon inked across his chest—his clan's sigil, intricate and primal—curls around his shoulder and down his arm, a mark of heritage and power.

But it's what's etched across his flesh that makes my breath catch.

Names.

More of them than before.

Written in ancient dragon script, flowing down his chest, curling around his ribs. Dark ink that seems to writhe in the candlelight.

"Nik, the marks—"

He's on me before I can finish, his mouth claiming mine in a kiss so desperate it steals my breath. His hands are everywhere, pulling me closer, silencing my questions with the heat of his body and the skill of his tongue.

I melt into him despite myself. Despite the fear curling in my chest. Despite knowing what those marks mean.

"How many—" I manage between feverish kisses.

"Not now." His voice is rough, edged with something between plea and command.

"Nik—"

"I need to be inside you." He shoves his pants down, and then he's naked and perfect and burning with barely controlled power. "Need to feel you around me. Need—" He stops, jaw clenching. "I need to claim you so badly it hurts."

And gods help me, I let him.

Because I'm under his spell. Completely. Utterly. The dragon's magic wraps around me like golden chains, and I surrender to it willingly.

"Then do it," I whisper. "Not the brand. Not yet. But this. Take this."

He's on me in an instant, spreading my thighs and settling between them. The head of his cock presses against my entrance, and we both groan at the contact.

"Tell me if it's too much," he says, even as he starts to push inside.

It's not too much. It's perfect.

He fills me in one long, slow thrust, and the stretch is delicious. I wrap my legs around his waist, drawing him deeper, and he curses.

"Gods." His forehead drops to mine. "You feel—Sam, you feel—"

"Move," I demand.

He does.

The careful lover from before is gone. This is the dragon. Rough and demanding and utterly dominant. He sets a brutal pace, each thrust driving me into the mattress. The headboard slams against the wall—too loud, definitely too loud—but neither of us can stop.

"Mine," he growls with each movement. "Mine, mine, mine."

"Yes," I gasp. "Yours."

His hand fists in my hair, tilting my head back to expose my throat. His teeth scrape my pulse point, and for a terrifying, thrilling moment, I think he might actually bite me. Claim me. Brand me despite everything.

"Please," I hear myself beg, though I'm not sure what I'm begging for.

"Not yet." But his voice is agonized. "Twenty days. Twenty fucking days and then I'm going to mark this throat. Going to make you wear my brand where everyone can see it. So they all know you're the Dragon Queen."

"Nik—"

"Kaisner thinks he can challenge me. Thinks he has a right to the title." Each word is punctuated by a thrust. "But when you're by my side, branded and crowned, there won't be any question. You're mine.

The throne is mine. And anyone who tries to take either from me will burn."

The possessiveness should probably worry me. Instead, it pushes me closer to the edge.

"I'm so close," I gasp.

"Good." His hand slides between us, finding me again. "Come with me... Want to feel you."

The combination of his hardness driving into me and his fingers on my clit sends me spiraling. I bury my face in his shoulder to muffle my scream as pleasure tears through me.

Nikolaas follows seconds later, his whole body going rigid as he comes. I feel the heat of him—hotter than normal, dragon-hot—and for a second, I glimpse gold scales ripple across his shoulders.

Then he collapses on top of me, breathing hard.

We lie there for a long moment, tangled together, his weight pressing me into the mattress. His skin is still burning, but it's cooling slowly. The gold in his eyes fading back to ice-blue.

"How many?" I ask quietly. My fingers trace the new marks on his chest. Three names I didn't recognize before. Fresh ink. Dark magic that feels cold against my fingertips.

He's silent for a long moment.

"Three," he finally says between panting breaths. "Since I got back from Scotland."

My heart clenches. "The grimoire—"

"Is giving me what I need." He catches my hand, stilling my tracing. "To secure the throne. To protect you. To make sure no one can challenge our claim when I brand you."

"Nik..." My voice breaks despite my efforts to stay calm. I'm beyond fighting him on this. Beyond arguing. At this point, I'm just desperate. Scared. "This is how it started with Willem. The death curses. The names. You told me about your ancestor—how the darkness consumed him—"

"I'm not Willem." He shifts, propping himself on his elbow to look down at me. His hand cups my face with devastating gentleness. "I know what I'm doing, Little Bear. I'm in control."

"Are you?" The question comes out small. Broken. "Because every time you come back from a trip, there are more marks. More names. And your eyes stay gold longer. Your dragon is closer to the surface. You're—" I swallow hard. "You're changing."

"I'm getting stronger." He brushes his thumb across my cheekbone, catching a tear I didn't know had fallen. "Everything I'm doing—the grimoire, the curses, all of it—it's for us. So we can be together without anyone threatening that. So I can make you my queen without Kaisner or anyone else trying to take you from me."

"I don't want to be a queen if it costs you your soul."

"It won't." He kisses me softly. Too softly. Like he's trying to erase my fears with tenderness. "I promise, Sam. Once the throne is secure. Once you're branded and crowned. Once Kaisner bends the knee or burns— I'll stop. The grimoire, the curses, all of it."

"You promise?"

"I swear it." His forehead drops to mine.

I want to believe him. Gods, I want to believe him so badly it hurts.

"I… almost bit you," he murmurs, voice rough with shame and residual want.

"I know."

"Would have branded you right there. Consequences be damned."

"I know." I run my fingers through his hair, soothing. "But you didn't. You controlled it."

"Barely." He lifts his head to look at me. "Baby, I don't know if I can wait twenty more days. My dragon is getting more insistent. More volatile."

I cup his face, searching those ice-blue eyes for the gold that's been bleeding through more and more lately.

A soft exhalation escapes him. "Tonight at the party—" He stops. "Kaisner will be there."

My stomach tightens. Kaisner Drachenstein. The other dragon shifter with a claim to the Dragon King title. Nik's rival. The man who stole Clarissa's heart. The man he'll have to fight—literally fight—to prove his right to rule.

"He won't start anything at Cassandra's party," I say, trying to sound confident.

"Won't he?" Nikolaas rolls off me, sitting on the edge of the bed with his head in his hands. "He knows how close we are to making this official. Knows that once I brand you, once you're my queen, his claim weakens. He might try something tonight. Might try to provoke me."

"Then don't let him." I sit up, wrapping my arms around him from behind. "You're stronger than this. Stronger than the dragon's demands."

"Am I?" He turns to look at me, and there's genuine fear in his eyes. "What if I'm not, Samara? What if I lose control at the party? What if I shift, or hurt someone, or—"

"You won't." I press a kiss to his shoulder. "Because I'll be there. And you don't lose control when I'm there."

"You're my anchor," he says quietly. "Just twenty more days. Then everything changes. I'll be Dragon King. You'll be my queen. And we won't need Willem's magic anymore."

He turns fully, cupping my face in his still-too-warm hands. "I love you."

"I love you too." I kiss him softly. "Now get dressed before Gavriil comes and finds you naked in my bed."

That gets a laugh out of him. He stands, pulling on his clothes with dragon-speed efficiency. By the time he's dressed, he looks almost normal. Except for the slight glow in his eyes. The way his skin still radiates heat.

"I'll meet you downstairs in an hour," he says. "We'll go to the party together."

"As long as you can keep your dragon in check."

"For you?" He steals one last kiss. "Anything."

Then he's gone, slipping out of my room with the stealth of someone who's done this before.

I collapse back on the bed, my body still humming with pleasure and my mind spinning with everything he said.

Twenty days until I can be his officially.

Twenty days until I become the Dragon Queen.

Twenty days until Kaisner has to face the reality that Nikolaas has won.

I just have to make sure we all survive tonight's party first.

Downstairs, I hear Gavriil's laughter echoing from his study. He sounds happy. Genuinely, completely happy in a way I haven't heard in years.

Luciana is good for him.

Maybe tonight won't be a disaster after all.

Maybe we can all gather, celebrate, choose each other despite the complications.

Maybe Christmas in May is exactly what we need.

I get up and reach for the crimson dress.

Time to get ready.

Time to be the future Dragon Queen, even if I can't wear the brand yet.

Time to stand beside Nikolaas as his anchor while he faces down his rival and fights for his throne.

Twenty days.

We can make it twenty days.

We have to.

9

CASSANDRA: LET THE CHAOS BEGIN

The Christmas tree is on fire.

Not metaphorically. *Actually* on fire. Small violet flames lick up the branches where I accidentally let my magic flare while hanging the last ornament.

"Dristan!" I call, trying not to panic. "The tree is—"

He's there in an instant, vampire-fast, wielding a fire extinguisher like it's a sword. White foam erupts across the lower branches, dousing my magical flames before they can spread to the black roses wound through the pine.

"Third time today," he observes mildly, setting down the extinguisher. "Should I just keep this nearby?"

"Probably." I sink onto the sofa, one hand on my six-month belly where the baby is kicking enthusiastically. As if applauding my latest magical disaster. "I don't know what's wrong with me. My control has never been this bad."

"You're six months pregnant with what is likely the most magically powerful baby in recent supernatural history." Dristan crouches in front of me, his ash-blonde hair falling into those ancient eyes. "Your magic has been fluctuating for weeks. It's normal."

"Normal would be nice." I gesture at the foam-covered tree. "This is my Christmas party, Dristan. The one I've been planning for weeks. The one that's supposed to prove I'm fine, we're fine, everything is fine. And I can't even hang ornaments without committing arson."

"Then don't hang ornaments." He takes my hands in his, cool vampire skin against my overheated palms. "Let me finish. You go get dressed. Try not to set anything else on fire."

"I make no promises."

But I let him pull me to my feet, let him kiss my forehead with that gentleness that still surprises me after everything. A thousand years old and he treats me like I'm made of glass.

I look around the great hall of Deveraux Manor. The tree—slightly singed but still magnificent. The black roses and silver bells. The gothic decorations that are somehow both elegant and absurd. The mistletoe hanging from every doorway—Dristan's reluctant handiwork from this morning.

"Last Christmas—" I start, then stop. He knows. He knows because he was there, kept away by Gavriil's brand, unable to reach me no matter how much he tried. "Last Christmas, I was alone. Branded. Pregnant and terrified. And I swore that if I survived, if we survived, I'd never let a holiday pass without celebrating everyone I love."

His grip on my hands tightens gently. "Even in May," he breathes with a smile.

"Timing doesn't matter," I add. "The calendar doesn't matter. What matters is that we're all here. All alive. All choosing each other despite everything that should tear us apart."

He's quiet for a moment, and when he speaks, his voice is rough. "You're extraordinary."

"I'm pregnant and setting things on fire."

"Both can be true." He steals another kiss. "Go. Get dressed. I'll handle the tree. And Cassandra?"

"Yes?"

"Thank you. For this. For inviting all of us into your chaos and calling it family."

My throat tightens with unexpected emotion. Damn pregnancy hormones. "You're welcome. Now go save my tree before I cry and set something else ablaze."

He laughs—rare and beautiful—and turns back to the decorating while I head upstairs.

An hour later, I'm standing in front of my mirror, smoothing down the deep purple velvet dress. Long sleeves, a sweetheart neckline that shows just enough, and a fitted silhouette that somehow manages to make my six-month pregnancy look regal instead of uncomfortable. The fabric clings and drapes in all the right places.

I secure my hair in a loose updo, letting a few dark strands frame my face, when I hear the unmistakable sound of the manor's front doors opening. The first guests have arrived.

Ivan's sardonic drawl reaches my ears before I see him. "Is that mistletoe? Everywhere? Cassandra, did you weaponize Christmas?"

"I lost that battle eight hours ago," Dristan replies from the hall.

"It's festive!" I call down the stairs.

"It's a lawsuit waiting to happen," Ivan shouts back.

But when I descend—carefully, because balance is a distant memory—I find him grinning. Juliette, beside him, looks radiant in emerald silk, her red hair swept up to reveal the elegant line of her neck. This is my ancestor, liberated from what she was three hundred years ago. No brand. No dragon's claim. Just her, free and choosing Ivan every single day.

"You look beautiful," Juliette says, embracing me carefully. "How are you feeling?"

"Like I might accidentally burn down my own party," I confess. "But otherwise excellent."

She squeezes my hand with fondness. "That's the spirit."

Ivan produces a bottle of wine—expensive, French, completely wasted on me since I can't drink. "For after," he says. "When you've survived hosting thirteen supernatural creatures for Christmas in May and need to question all your life choices."

I snort. "You're assuming we'll survive."

"Optimism is my brand." Ivan spreads his hands, the picture of false innocence.

I raise an eyebrow. "Your brand is sardonic pessimism wrapped in expensive suits."

He smooths his lapels with obvious satisfaction. "That too."

Dristan joins us, and the two of them exchange that particular look—maker and fledgling, three hundred years of history in a glance. Then Dristan steals Ivan's wine and heads to the kitchen, and Ivan's protest follows him down the hall.

"They're good together," Juliette observes. "In their way."

"They're ridiculous," I correct. "But yes."

The next arrivals are a study in contrasts. Gavriil enters like he owns the place—which, given our complicated family alliance, he sort of does. Ursa King, recently reunited with Luciana, looking happier than I've ever seen him. The blonde woman at his side is delicate and lovely, violet eyes bright with curiosity as she takes in the decorations.

"Cassandra." Gavriil's voice is formal, but there's warmth beneath it. "Thank you for inviting us."

"Thank you for coming." I mean it. Five months ago, he branded me. Forced a magical bond that kept Dristan away and nearly destroyed us both. But he also gave me the power to bring Luciana back. To break free. To survive.

Forgiveness is complicated.

"The decorations are beautiful," Luciana says, and her smile is genuine. "Christmas in May. I love it."

"It's absurd," Gavriil mutters.

"It's perfect," she corrects, kissing his cheek.

Behind them, Samara and Nikolaas arrive, and the temperature in the room immediately rises. Literally. The dragon shifter radiates heat, his ice-blue eyes scanning the space like he's cataloging threats. Samara's hand is locked in his, her knuckles white with tension.

"Nikolaas. Samara." I greet them warmly, pretending not to notice the way his eyes flash gold when he looks at the mistletoe. "I'm so glad you could make it."

"Wouldn't miss it," Samara says, but her smile doesn't reach her eyes. She's worried about something. About him, probably. The dragon looks wound tight enough to snap.

"Bar's in the parlor," Dristan offers. "Help yourself to whatever you need."

"Perfect." Nikolaas heads that direction immediately, Samara trailing after him.

"Is he alright?" I ask quietly, watching Nikolaas head toward the parlor.

Gavriil's expression darkens. "His dragon is volatile. Has been for weeks. Kaisner's been making moves. Challenging his claim."

My stomach drops. "And Kaisner's coming tonight."

"Mm." Gavriil's jaw tightens.

I glance toward the parlor where Nikolaas disappeared. "Should I be worried?"

"Always." His tone is grim. Gavriil's hand settles briefly on my shoulder—protective, almost brotherly. "But we'll handle it. You focus on your party."

Easier said than done.

The next arrivals are Vlad—Gavriil's brother—with his mate Anya and their daughter Katya. Vlad carries a bottle in each hand, grinning.

"Real vodka," he announces. "Not that French nonsense. Where should I put these?"

"Kitchen," Dristan directs. "Thank you."

Anya sets Katya down, and the toddler immediately toddles toward the Christmas tree on unsteady legs, silver eyes wide with wonder. She squeals with delight, tiny hands reaching, and her magic responds—fresh mistletoe blooming across the ceiling in enthusiastic bursts.

"Katya, no!" Anya tries to catch her, but the little wolf-witch is surprisingly fast for someone who just learned to walk. "Baby, we talked about this—"

Too late. The entire great hall is now carpeted in green and white.

"It's fine," I laugh, watching Katya plop down on her bottom in amazement at what she's created. "It's perfect. *She's* perfect."

The toddler grins up at me, showing tiny teeth, and makes it snow indoors.

"Katya!"

But the snow is gentle. Magical. Beautiful in a way that makes my chest ache. This. This is what I wanted. Chaos and magic and family choosing to show up for each other.

Clarissa and Kaisner arrive last. Even with all the complications between us, I'm genuinely happy to see them both.

"Kaisner!" I move to greet my childhood friend, and he pulls me into a careful hug that accounts for my belly.

"Cass." His maroon eyes are warm, affectionate. "You look radiant. Christmas in May? Only you would pull off something this brilliantly absurd."

"I learned from the best chaos-maker I know."

"Flatterer," he scoffs, but he's grinning as he releases me, stepping back to let Clarissa through.

"Clarissa." I embrace the youngest Draken sibling. She's family—has been since the Yule dinner when everything exploded, and they all stayed anyway. When they all chose to protect my secret, to stand with us. "How are you?"

"Nervous," she admits, her seer's eyes flickering with something distant. Worried. "There are a lot of futures converging tonight, Cassie. A lot of paths that could go very wrong."

"But some that go right?" I try to sound hopeful.

"Some." She manages a smile. "Your baby helps. Their presence seems to... quiet the noise. The thousand branching futures narrow down to the ones that matter most."

"Well, that's good news."

Kaisner's gaze sweeps the room, and I notice the slight shift in his expression. Dragon recognizing dragon, even from different rooms. The air itself feels charged with competing fire.

"He's in the parlor, isn't he?" Kaisner asks quietly.

"Yes." I touch his arm. "But Kaisner, please—"

"I'm not here to fight, Cass." But his expression is serious now, that controlled intensity settling over him. "I'm here for you. Because you invited me. Because we're family." He glances toward the parlor. "But I should say hello. Establish that we can be civil."

"Can you?" I ask bluntly.

"For you? For Clarissa and Samara?" He squeezes my hand. "Yes. But Nik has to meet me halfway."

He heads toward the parlor, and Clarissa stays beside me, watching him go with those haunted seer's eyes.

"This is going to be… complicated," she murmurs.

"Everything with dragons is complicated," I reply.

"True." She looks at me, and for a moment, her gift seems to clear. "But you're doing something important here, Cassandra. Gathering everyone. Choosing celebration over fear. It matters more than you know."

"Even if it ends in disaster?"

"Even then."

I exchange a worried look with Dristan, who's appeared silently at my side. He wraps an arm around my waist, his hand settling over where the baby kicks.

"This is going to be a disaster," I murmur.

"Probably." His voice is calm, steady. "But it's your disaster. And we're all here for it."

I lean into him, drawing strength from his steady presence. Around us, the party is taking shape. Ivan and Juliette laughing with Vlad. Gavriil and Luciana examining the tree. Samara hovering near the parlor door, ready to intervene if the dragons clash. Clarissa silent in the corner, eyes tracking timelines none of the rest of us can see.

My family. Chosen. Complicated. Absolutely chaotic.

Perfect.

"Alright," I announce, raising my voice over the conversations. "Everyone's here. Dinner's ready. And before anyone asks—yes, we're doing Secret Santa. Yes, in May. No, I don't care that it makes no sense. This is my Christmas party, and we're celebrating."

"Hear, hear," Ivan raises a glass. "To Cassandra's questionable life choices and our collective willingness to enable them."

"To Christmas in May," Juliette adds.

"To family," Dristan says quietly, and his hand tightens on my waist.

"To survival," Gavriil mutters, but he's smiling.

And as everyone raises their glasses and drinks, as little Katya makes mistletoe bloom and my magic flickers violet at the edges of my vision, I think:

We might actually pull this off.

We might actually have our Christmas in May without everything falling apart.

The baby lands a solid kick. I'll take that as a no.

As if on cue, in the parlor, I hear the first rumble of dragon fire as Nikolaas and Kaisner face each other.

Or not.

"Dinner!" I call brightly. "Everyone to the dining room before the dragons destroy my house!"

Because if we're going to have a disaster, we might as well do it over a good meal.

Dristan laughs and guides me toward the dining room, and behind us, I hear Ivan mutter to Juliette:

"I give it twenty minutes before something catches fire."

"Fifteen," she corrects.

"Ten," Gavriil adds.

"You're all terrible," I call back.

But I'm smiling.

Because they're here. All of them. Despite the danger. Despite the drama. Despite knowing that putting Nikolaas and Kaisner in the same room might end in bloodshed.

They came.

For me. For each other. For this absurd celebration of chosen family and impossible timing.

And that's worth any disaster that might follow.

10

GAVRIIL: SECRET SANTA

Dinner is chaos.

The good kind, mostly. Laughter echoing off ancient walls. My niece—my brother's precious cub—making snowflakes appear in her mashed potatoes while Anya tries to convince her to eat instead of enchant. Katya looks up at me and giggles, and despite the weight of what I need to do tonight, I feel my chest warm with pride. Our family's future, sitting right there in a high chair, commanding winter like she was born to it. Vlad arguing with Ivan about the proper way to age vodka. Juliette and Luciana deep in conversation about resurrection magic, their voices low and intimate.

Our usual normal. Almost.

Except for the millenary vampire sitting directly across from me, his ancient eyes tracking my every movement with the cold precision of a predator contemplating murder.

Dristan hasn't looked away from me since we sat down.

Not once.

I don't blame him.

Five months ago, I branded his mate. Forced a magical bond on Cassandra that kept him away from her, unable to reach her, no matter how desperately he tried. Watched her suffer alone, pregnant and terrified, while my spell prevented him from crossing the threshold of her home.

That he hasn't tried to kill me yet proves only Cassandra's influence.

Or perhaps he's simply waiting for the right moment—I know *I* would.

"You're tense," Luciana murmurs beside me, her hand finding mine under the table. Warm. Grounding. The woman I thought I'd lost forever, brought back to life by the very witch whose brand I forced into existence.

"Just thinking."

"About the gift?"

My hand moves unconsciously to my jacket pocket, where the wrapped grimoire sits like a lead weight. "Among other things."

Her violet eyes—so like Juliette's, yet wholly her own—soften with understanding. "He won't forgive you easily. Maybe not ever."

"I know."

"But *she* has." Luciana squeezes my fingers. "Cassandra forgave you. That has to count for something."

"Does it?" I glance at Dristan again. He's holding his wine glass with deliberate stillness, but I can see the tension in his shoulders. The way his jaw clenches every time I speak. "I kept him from his mate. Tortured him by keeping her just out of reach. If someone had done that to me—" I stop, because the thought of being separated from Luciana again, of having her so close but unable to touch her, makes rage coil in my chest like a living thing. "I would have burned the world down."

"And yet you sit here, alive and whole." She leans closer, her voice dropping. "Because Cassandra asked him not to. Because, despite everything you did, she chose to forgive. To move forward. To call you family."

Family.

The word sits strangely in my mouth. I have siblings—Samara, Vlad, and Anya. My clan. My pack. But this? This chosen collection of supernatural creatures gathered around a table in May, celebrating Christmas because one pregnant witch decided timing doesn't matter?

This is something else entirely.

"Alright!" Cassandra calls out, her voice cutting through the conversations. She's glowing—literally, violet magic radiating at the edges as the baby's power responds to her joy. "Before dessert, we're doing Secret Santa. Everyone drew names a few weeks ago. Time to see what chaos you've all created."

Groans and laughter ripple around the table.

"As the hostess of this evening," Cassandra says,

rising from her seat with one hand steadying herself on Dristan's shoulder, "I'll start."

She produces a small velvet box from beneath her chair—deep purple, tied with silver ribbon. I watch as she crosses to where Juliette sits beside Ivan, radiant in her emerald silk.

"Juliette," Cassandra begins, and her voice catches slightly. "When I drew your name, I kept thinking about what you could possibly want. You jumped three centuries to be here. What do you give someone who left everything behind to reach this moment?"

Juliette's amethyst eyes gleam with curiosity.

"Then I realized—you didn't just travel through time. You came home. To us. To the Deveraux line that blossomed thanks to you, that continued after you cast that spell and waited."

Cassandra places the box in Juliette's elegant hands.

"This was my mother's. And her mother's before her. The Deveraux women passed it down for generations—every one of us descended from you." She watches as Juliette opens it carefully. Inside rests an antique locket, silver with amethyst stones. "It's been waiting. For the woman it was always meant for."

Juliette lifts the locket with trembling fingers. When she opens it, I see two miniature portraits inside—one of Juliette in the seventeenth century, young and uncertain, and one that must have been painted recently of her now.

"Past and present," Cassandra whispers. "The woman you were and the woman you are. Your journey through time. Because you made it, Juliette. You're here. And this is your time. Your moment."

Tears slip down Juliette's porcelain cheeks. She stands, pulling Cassandra into an embrace fierce enough that even from here I can see the awkwardness of navigating around Cassandra's pregnant belly.

"Mon cœur," Juliette whispers. "Cassandra, this is... this is so beautiful."

When they finally separate, Juliette fastens the locket around her neck immediately, her fingers touching it like a talisman.

"Thank you," she says, voice thick with emotion. "For honoring both who I was and who I've become."

Cassandra returns to her seat, Dristan pulling her close. Across the table, Juliette keeps touching the locket like she's afraid it might disappear. Like all of this might disappear—this family, this time, this life she fought three hundred years to reach.

"I'm next," Juliette says, composing herself. She produces a small wooden box carved with intricate wolf motifs and hands it to Vlad. "Ever since I drew your name, I've been searching for this. Luckily, I found it just in time."

Vlad opens it carefully, and his silver eyes widen. Inside, nestled on black velvet, is a silver pendant—a wolf running free beneath a full moon, the craftsmanship exquisite, ancient.

"This is—" His voice catches. "This is Volkov clan work. Pre-Revolution Russian silverwork."

"From your original pack," Juliette confirms softly.

"Before they cast you out. Before Gavriil's father found you wandering the forests and brought you home." She pauses, letting the weight of history settle between them. "I wanted to give you something to remind you that the shadows of your past don't define your future. You're not the runt they abandoned, Vladimir. You're the true Volkov alpha. And you have the power to write your clan's story however you choose."

The silence that follows is profound.

Vlad stares at the pendant, his jaw working as he fights for composure. When he finally looks up at Juliette, there's something raw and vulnerable in his expression—the runt who was left to die, now a man who leads with the strength his birth pack never saw in him.

"How did you find this?" he asks, voice barely above a whisper.

"I have my ways." Her smile is gentle, understanding. "You're family, Vlad. To all of us. Not because of blood or pack law, but because you chose us and we chose you. I wanted you to know that."

He stands abruptly, crossing to her in two strides. The embrace he pulls her into is brief but fierce—the kind of gratitude that goes beyond words. "Thank you," he says against her hair. "This means more than you know."

When he releases her, he takes a moment to compose himself. Clears his throat. Tucks the precious box carefully into his jacket pocket, where it rests against his heart.

"I guess it's my turn now," he says, his voice steadier. He looks across the table at Anya, and his silver eyes soften in a way I've only ever seen when he looks at her or their child. "The person I drew is the woman who gave me something I never thought I'd have. Not just a daughter—though Katya is the greatest gift I've ever received—but *a home*. A future. A reason to be more than what my past tried to make me."

Anya's breath catches, her hand flying to her mouth.

Vlad produces a velvet box, then glances down at Katya, who's abandoned her enchanted potatoes to watch her father with wide, curious eyes.

"Come here, little wolf," he says gently, crouching to her level. "Help Papa give Mama her present."

Katya squeals with delight, her tiny hands reaching for the box. Vlad places it carefully in her grip, steadying her as she takes her first wobbly steps away from her high chair.

The room goes silent, watching.

She toddles toward Anya—unsteady, determined, magic sparking at her fingertips, making small flowers bloom in the air around her with each step. One foot, then the other. Her little face scrunched in concentration.

"That's it, *printsessa*," Anya whispers, tears already forming. "Come to Mama."

Katya makes it three more steps before she stumbles. Vlad is there instantly, catching her, but she giggles and pushes at his hands. "No, Papa! Me do it!"

He releases her, and she completes the journey on

her own, crashing into Anya's waiting arms with the box clutched triumphantly in her chubby fists.

"Good girl," Anya laughs through tears, kissing her daughter's dark hair. "Such a good, strong girl."

Katya presents the box with all the solemnity a toddler can muster. "For you, Mama!"

Anya opens it with trembling hands, and when she sees what's inside, her tears spill over. A necklace— delicate silver with a moonstone pendant that catches the candlelight like captured starlight.

"It was my mother's," Vlad says quietly, coming to stand behind them both. "The only thing I had left of her. The only thing they let me take when they..." He stops, swallows hard. "She would have wanted you to have it. Would have loved you. Loved Katya. Loved the family we've built from the ashes of what was."

Anya stands, baby Katya on her hip, and kisses him. Deep and full of emotion.

"I love you," she whispers against his lips. "Both of you. All of us."

Katya claps her tiny hands, and snowflakes drift down from the ceiling—slow and gentle, catching the candlelight as they fall.

Anya takes a moment to compose herself, wiping her eyes before turning to the table. The moonstone pendant now rests against her throat, casting rainbows with every breath.

"My turn," she says softly, her accent thickening with emotion the way it does when she's deeply moved. She reaches beneath her chair and produces a beautifully wrapped package, crossing to where Samara sits beside Nikolaas.

"When I drew your name," Anya begins, her voice steady despite the tears still glistening in her eyes, "I thought about what I could possibly give the woman who has everything. The Ursa Princess who commands winter and fire with equal grace. The future Dragon Queen."

I instantly go rigid. Nikolaas' claim, delivered so casually. I want to believe Anya spoke from the heart and not from calculated strategy. The effect, however, remains unchanged.

A quick glance is enough to see Kaisner's jaw tighten in response.

Anya pauses, kneeling beside Samara's chair so they're eye to eye. "But then I realized—you're not just that to me. You're the sister I never had."

Samara's breath catches.

"I grew up alone," Anya continues. "An only child in a pack that valued family above all else. I watched other girls grow up with sisters—sharing secrets, braiding hair, standing beside each other through every trial. I envied that. Ached for it." She places the package in Samara's hands. "And then Vlad brought me into this family. Into *your* family. And you didn't just accept me, Sam. You chose me. You taught me how to navigate bear politics when I had no idea what I was doing. You held Katya when she was hours old and swore you'd protect her with your life. You've been the sister I always dreamed of having."

Samara's eyes are bright with unshed tears, her usual composure cracking.

"So this is for you," Anya says. "Not for the Ursa Princess or the future Dragon Queen. It's for my sister."

The title echoes through the room again, impossible to unhear even as she dismisses it. I wince inwardly. My sister, on the other hand, is terribly moved.

"Oh, Anya..." she chokes out.

Samara opens the package with trembling hands. Inside is a hand-embroidered shawl—intricate, beautiful, clearly made with painstaking care. The pattern shows the phases of the moon in silver thread, each phase perfectly rendered, from new moon to full and back again.

"I made it myself," Anya admits. "Every stitch. It took me three weeks. The moon phases—they're the emblem of the Ursa clan. Your clan. But they're sacred to wolf shifters too, woven into our oldest lore." She touches the silver thread carefully, tracing the full moon at the center. "I wanted to create something that honored both our heritages. A symbol of unity. Of what we've become together—not wolf or bear, but family. Sisters who chose each other despite coming from different packs, different bloods."

She points to delicate winter roses embroidered around the edges. "These are for Katya. Because she's the future we're building. The next generation that won't see wolf and bear as separate, but as one family united under the same moon."

Samara stands abruptly, pulling Anya into a fierce embrace. "Sister," she whispers, voice breaking. "My sister."

They hold each other for a long moment, and something tight loosens in my chest.

My sister. My brother's mate. Two women who should have been strangers, brought together by circumstance and choice. Watching them embrace, fierce protectiveness and gratitude surge within me.

This.

Clan. Pack. *This* is what family should be.

Not forced bonds or political alliances—though those have their place. But this kind of love. The kind that's chosen. Earned. Built stitch by painstaking stitch over months and years.

Across from me, Vlad watches his mate and my sister with quiet satisfaction, and I catch his eye. He nods once, understanding passing between us without words. *We did well. We built something good here.*

Even Nikolaas looks moved, his hand finding Samara's shoulder when they finally separate, grounding her as she struggles to compose herself.

The gesture is genuine. I can see it in the careful way he touches her, the softness in his expression. This is the man my sister loves.

But Vlad's words echo in my mind: *Watch her. Really watch.* And I do. I see the way Samara leans into that touch—not with joy, but with relief. Like she's been waiting for this version of him to return. Like she never knows how long it will last. Twenty days until she turns twenty-one. Twenty days to decide if I let her bind herself to this.

"This is—Anya. This is perfect," Samara manages, clutching the shawl with fondness. Her voice breaks on the words. "I love you."

"I love you too." Anya grins through her tears, reaching up to cup Samara's face with sisterly affection.

Luciana's hand finds mine beneath the table, squeezing gently. She knows. She sees what this means to me—watching my family grow, watching love multiply instead of fracture.

This is why I did what I did. Why I forced that brand. To protect this. To build this.

Even if the cost was too high.

Samara takes a moment to compose herself, carefully folding the shawl and draping it around her shoulders. The silver moon phases catch the light, and I feel a surge of pride watching my sister wear Anya's gift like the treasure it is.

"I'm next," Samara says, her voice still thick with emotion. She produces a wooden box—ornate, ancient—and slides it across the table to Clarissa. "I know you've been searching for this."

The youngest Draken sibling opens it with reverent care, and even from here, I can see her hands trembling. When she lifts the lid, her pale blue eyes go wide, filling with tears that threaten to spill over.

"The Marseille deck," she breathes. "The original 1760 edition." Her fingers hover over the cards as if afraid they might disappear if she touches them. "Sam, I've been trying to find this for *months*. How did you—"

"I remembered." Samara's smile is soft, genuine. "When we went shopping that day. You mentioned it in passing, but I could tell how much it mattered to you. So, I started asking around. Called in a few favors."

Clarissa looks up at her, and something passes between them that makes my chest tighten. Not just gratitude. Understanding. The recognition that someone listened. Someone remembered. Someone cared enough to track down a single deck of cards because it would bring joy.

That's family. The real kind.

"This means everything," Clarissa whispers, standing to embrace Samara. "Thank you. Thank you so much."

When they separate, Clarissa clutches the box to her chest like it contains her heart. Maybe it does. Seers and their tools—I've never fully understood the bond, but I recognize devotion when I see it.

She returns to her seat, setting the box carefully beside her plate. Then she takes a breath—the kind that suggests she's steeling herself for something difficult—and produces a small wrapped package.

"Nikolaas," she says quietly, and the entire room shifts.

I feel it. The way the temperature rises slightly. The way Nikolaas tenses in his chair, his ice-blue eyes flashing gold for just a moment before he wrestles his dragon back under control. The way Kaisner goes still across the table, watching.

The siblings haven't spoken properly since the confrontation at this very manor months ago. Since Clarissa chose to stand by Kaisner despite Nikolaas' fury. Since their family fractured along fault lines that have existed for generations.

"I drew your name," Clarissa continues, and there's something vulnerable in her voice. Pleading, almost. "I know things have been... difficult between us. But you're still my brother. You'll always be my brother."

Nikolaas doesn't move. Doesn't reach for the gift. His jaw is clenched so tight I can see the muscle jumping, and his hands are flat on the table like he's physically holding himself in place.

Samara's hand finds his shoulder. Anchoring him. Reminding him to breathe.

Clarissa stands, crossing to him with careful steps. She sets the package directly in front of him, then does something that makes my throat tighten— she places her hand over his, a gesture of connection they're still learning how to forge after being separated so young.

"I'm sorry," she whispers, and it's so quiet I almost miss it. "For hurting you. For choosing him when you asked me not to. For everything."

Nikolaas's eyes close. A shudder runs through him —dragon fire barely contained beneath mortal skin.

"I don't regret loving Kaisner," Clarissa says, and across the table, Kaisner's expression goes carefully blank. "But I regret how it wounded you. How it made you feel like I was choosing him over you. Over our family." Her voice breaks. "You're my brother, Nik. My protector. The person who taught me everything about what it means to be a Draken. Nothing—not even love—could ever replace that."

The silence is profound. Suffocating.

Then Nikolaas opens his eyes, and I see the gold receding. The man wrestling the dragon back into submission through sheer force of will. Admirable progress, considering the rumors of the curse running underneath his skin.

"Open it," Clarissa urges softly. "Please."

His hands move slowly, mechanically. Unwrapping the paper with precision that reveals rigid control. Inside is a leather journal—old, worn, clearly well-loved.

"It's Father's," Clarissa explains, her voice trembling. "His private journal from the year before he died. Before the fire." She stops, swallows hard. The fire Nikolaas started. The fire that killed their parents. Everyone at this table knows the story—the first fire-gifted dragon shifter the Draken family had seen in centuries, manifesting his power as a child with devastating consequences. "There are entries about you. About your fire magic. About how proud he was."

Nikolaas stares at the journal like it's made of living fire.

"I found it in the archives last month," Clarissa continues, her voice barely above a whisper. "I've been reading it. Trying to understand what he went through as the leader of our clan. The burden he carried, like you do now." Her hand tightens on his. "There are pages and pages about you, Nik. About watching your fire magic develop. About how extraordinary you were. How proud he was of the power you were showing, even so young. He called you his 'little flame.' Said you were going to change everything for our family."

A sound escapes Nikolaas—half sob, half gasp.

"He loved you," Clarissa says fiercely. "He was proud of you. Not afraid. Not disappointed. *Proud*. And he would still be proud now. Of the man you've become. Of how you've mastered the fire that—" She stops, choosing her words carefully. "Of how you've turned tragedy into strength. You have Samara. You have all of us. And I believe in you. I've always believed in you."

Something breaks.

I see it happen—the moment Nikolaas's control shatters not into rage but into grief. He stands abruptly, pulling Clarissa into his arms with desperate force. His shoulders shake, and I realize with a jolt that he's crying. The Dragon Prince. The man who never shows weakness. Crying into his sister's hair while she holds him and whispers things I can't hear.

Samara's eyes glisten with tears, her hand pressed to her mouth.

Across the table, Kaisner watches with an expression I can't quite read. Pain, maybe. Guilt. Understanding that he's the wedge that drove these siblings apart, even if Clarissa chose him willingly.

"I'm sorry too," Nikolaas finally manages, his voice wrecked. "For being angry. For not trusting your choice. For making you feel like you had to choose between us." He pulls back just enough to look at her. "You're my sister. *My* Rissy. Nothing could ever change that."

"Brothers?" Clarissa asks, using the childhood term they haven't spoken in months.

"Always," Nikolaas promises. "Even when I'm being an overprotective idiot."

"Then, most of all."

They embrace again, and I feel Luciana's hand find mine beneath the table. When I glance at her, there are tears tracking down her cheeks.

"Family," she whispers. "Choosing each other despite the pain. That's what matters."

I nod, unable to speak past the tightness in my throat.

Because I understand now—really understand— why Cassandra fought so hard to break my brand. Why Dristan would have burned the world to reach her. Why these moments of choosing each other, of forgiveness and reconciliation, matter more than any political alliance or magical bond.

Love isn't something you can force.

It's something you build. Stitch by painstaking stitch. Gift by gift. Apology by apology. Choice by choice.

When Nikolaas and Clarissa finally separate, there's

something lighter in the room. As if a weight we'd all been carrying has lifted slightly.

Nikolaas moves back toward his seat, the journal clutched in his hands like a lifeline. He looks at Clarissa with such profound gratitude that I have to look away, feeling like I'm intruding on something sacred.

He remains standing, and I see him transform. See him pull the Dragon Prince mask back into place—controlled, powerful, regal. But there's something different now. Something softer beneath the armor. He takes a breath, steadying himself. He produces his own gift—a slim box wrapped in midnight blue—and turns to face his rival.

The temperature in the room drops.

Kaisner meets his gaze steadily, dark maroon eyes unreadable.

"Kaisner," Nikolaas says, and his voice is carefully neutral. "I drew your name."

The irony isn't lost on anyone. The two dragon shifters fighting for the same crown. The same throne. The same future. And fate—or Cassandra's velvet bag —has decided they must exchange gifts.

"Of course you did," Kaisner replies, equally controlled. "The gods have a sense of humor."

"Apparently."

Nikolaas crosses to him, and every person at the table tenses. Ready to intervene if dragon fire erupts. If this fragile peace shatters into violence.

But Nikolaas simply sets the box in front of Kaisner and steps back.

"I spent three days looking for this," he says quietly. "Not because I like you. Not because I accept your claim to my throne." He pauses, and something raw flickers in his expression. "But because my sister loves you. And that means something. Whether I want it to or not."

Kaisner opens the box with deliberate care.

Inside is a compass. Antique, beautifully crafted, the kind that costs a fortune and carries history in every scratch and dent.

"It belonged to the first Draken who sailed from the Netherlands to establish our line in France," Nikolaas explains. "1543. Cornelis Van Draken used it to navigate between worlds—mortal and supernatural. To find his way home when everything else was uncertain."

He meets Kaisner's eyes, and something passes between them that I don't fully grasp.

"We're both lost right now," Nikolaas says. "Both trying to navigate waters that want to drown us. Both fighting for a future that might destroy us." His voice drops. "You're Drachenstein. I'm Draken. We come from rival clans, rival nations, rival bloodlines. We should be enemies by birthright alone."

He pauses, and the gravity of what he's offering settles over the room.

"But you love my sister. And she loves you. That makes you..." He struggles with the word, jaw clenching. "That makes you family. Whether I want it to or not."

Kaisner stares at the compass, his expression unreadable.

"I'm giving you this," Nikolaas continues, "as a symbol. The Draken compass, offered to a Drachenstein. A reminder that even rival clans can find common ground. That even enemies can navigate toward the same home."

Kaisner's hand trembles—just slightly, barely perceptible—as his fingers close around the compass. His maroon eyes lock onto Nikolaas, and for a moment, the controlled Drachenstein heir falters. I see his throat work as he swallows hard, see the way his jaw clenches like he's fighting to maintain composure.

"You honor me," Kaisner says quietly, and there's something raw in his voice. Something grateful and pained all at once. He starts to rise, perhaps to embrace him, to bridge the distance—

But Nikolaas takes a step back, and the moment shatters.

"I don't forgive you for making Clarissa a target. I don't accept your claim to the Dragon King throne. I will fight you for it when the time comes, and I will win." His voice hardens. "But tonight, in this place, with these people who somehow became family... I can acknowledge that you're not just my rival. You're the man my sister chose. And her choice matters to me, even if you don't."

The silence stretches.

Then Kaisner steps forward, and for a terrifying

moment, I think he might attack. Might let his dragon rise to meet the challenge in Nikolaas' words.

My bear surges to the surface instantly. I sense my muscles coil, ready to shift, ready to protect. Luciana is beside me. Samara across the table. Cassandra, carrying the most powerful child in supernatural history—a child I swore to protect.

My family. My pack. If dragon fire erupts, I will end it.

Vlad tenses beside me—his silver eyes flash wolf-bright. Even Dristan goes utterly still, that vampire stillness that precedes violence.

The room holds its breath.

But instead of attacking, Kaisner offers his hand.

"I appreciate it," Kaisner says quietly. "The gift. The grace. Not burning down Cassandra's Christmas party despite every instinct telling you to challenge me."

Nikolaas takes his hand, and their grips are equally firm. Equally controlled. A handshake that's as much threat as truce.

"Do *not* mistake this for friendship," Nikolaas warns.

"I wouldn't dream of it."

"Good."

They release each other, and both dragons step back, returning to their seats—guardedly, fully aware of each other. The room exhales collectively, tension easing but not disappearing.

Samara's hand immediately finds Nikolaas',

steadying him. Clarissa's gaze flickers from her brother to her mate with cautious hope.

And I sit back, marveling at what I just witnessed.

Two dragons who should be enemies, exchanging gifts with something approaching respect.

A sister who mended a wound she didn't entirely cause.

A family that's choosing each other despite every reason to fracture.

A truce—at least for now.

11

GAVRIIL: ABSOLUTION

Kaisner remains standing, his hand still resting on the compass like it's a talisman. He takes a breath, composing himself with visible effort, then reaches into his jacket and produces a small velvet pouch.

"Luciana," he says, turning to face her with that careful courtesy he seems to reserve for those he respects. "I drew your name."

Luciana sits up straighter, surprise flickering across her delicate features. "You did?"

"I did." He crosses to her, and I feel myself tense automatically—protective instinct rising—but his posture is respectful, unthreatening. He places the pouch gently in front of her. "I understand you've recently been... *restored*." His eyes meet Cassandra's briefly. "Brought back from death through magic that shouldn't exist."

Luciana nods slowly, her violet eyes curious.

"I know something about resurrection," Kaisner continues quietly. "About being given a second chance at life when everything should have been over." His maroon eyes hold shadows I don't fully understand. "It changes you. Makes you question everything. Makes you wonder if you deserve the gift you've been given."

Luciana's hand finds mine beneath the table, squeezing tight.

"So I wanted to give you something," Kaisner says, "that reminded you that you do. That you deserve every moment of this second life. Every breath. Every joy."

She opens the pouch with trembling fingers, and inside is a delicate bracelet—violet stones set in gold, each one catching the candlelight like captured starlight.

"Amethyst," Kaisner explains. "In ancient lore, it's the stone of rebirth. Of transformation. Of turning grief into beauty." He pauses. "Each stone represents a presence that played a part in pulling you back from death. Magic. Love. Grief. Life." His voice softens. "Souls woven together to defy death itself."

I count them silently. Six stones.

Cassandra. Her unborn child. Ivan. Juliette. Kelham. And me.

Not me in the flesh—I wasn't there that night. But my grief was. Channeled through the brand I'd forced on Cassandra, my sorrow became the bridge that brought Luciana home.

Six souls bound to resurrection.

"Kaisner," Luciana whispers, her voice thick with emotion. "This is—I don't know what to say."

"Say you'll wear it," he replies simply. "Say you'll remember that you're not a ghost. Not borrowed time. You're alive. Truly alive. And that matters."

She stands, and before I can process what's happening, she's embracing him. Brief but genuine. "Thank you," she says against his shoulder.

When she releases him and returns to her seat, I see tears tracking down her cheeks. She fastens the bracelet around her wrist immediately, and the violet stones catch the light, making her eyes seem even brighter.

"It's perfect," she says, looking at Kaisner with such gratitude that something loosens in my chest. I cannot say I share this understanding of being restored into life, but the dragon shifter clearly does.

He nods once, then returns to his seat beside Clarissa, who takes his hand with obvious pride.

Luciana takes a steadying breath, touching the bracelet like it's precious beyond measure. Then she reaches beneath her chair and produces a wrapped bottle—elegant, expensive.

"Ivan," she says, and the vampire's eyebrows rise in surprise. "I believe you're next."

"Am I?" Ivan's sardonic smile appears. "How delightful. And here I thought you'd forgotten me."

"Never." She rises, crossing to him with that ethereal grace that makes her seem like she's gliding rather than walking. "I drew your name weeks ago and have been planning this ever since."

She sets the bottle in front of him, and when he unwraps it, his expression shifts from amusement to genuine shock.

"1811 Château d'Yquem," he breathes. "Luciana, this is—this bottle shouldn't even exist. The vintage was nearly destroyed in—"

"I know." Her smile is mysterious. "Let's just say I have... connections. From before."

Before she died. Before she spent a year as a ghost, watching the world move on without her.

Ivan stands, pulling her into a careful embrace. "This is extraordinary."

"I'm glad you approve." She pulls back, her eyes serious. "You've been good to Juliette. You love her with a devotion that transcends time itself—through her death, through centuries of waiting, through resurrection and reunion."

"I try," Ivan says, and there's genuine warmth in his voice. "She makes it easy."

Juliette watches from across the table, her amethyst eyes soft with affection for them both.

"That kind of love..." Luciana's voice softens with admiration. "That deserves something extraordinary."

Ivan returns to his seat, cradling the bottle like the treasure it is, and Juliette reaches for his hand across the table—a silent acknowledgment of what Luciana just said.

"So, I guess I'm next," the vampire announces,

producing an elegantly wrapped box. He turns to me with that sardonic smile.

Gods, no. Please, no.

"Gavriil," the bastard pauses for effect. "I drew your name and spent far too much time trying to find the perfect balance of thoughtful and mildly insulting."

"Of course you did," I mutter, accepting the box.

Inside is a smart home AI hub—sleek, expensive, top-of-the-line. Exactly the kind of tech I love. But there's also a bear-shaped USB drive.

"The AI comes pre-programmed," Ivan explains, looking far too pleased with himself. "With custom responses."

I plug in the USB, and the AI activates.

"Good evening, Your Majesty," it says in Ivan's sardonic drawl. *"The lights are on. Try not to trip over your own ego."*

The table erupts in laughter.

"I absolutely hate you," I say, but I'm fighting a smile.

"You're welcome." Ivan grins. "There are about fifty more responses. All equally delightful."

"I can imagine," I mutter, putting away the damned thing.

"Gavriil," Cassandra says, turning those violet eyes on me. "You're next."

The room goes quiet.

Everyone knows I drew her name. Luciana told me she'd accidentally let it slip to Juliette, who told Ivan, who told everyone because vampires can't keep secrets to save their immortal lives.

Which means everyone knows this moment is coming.

Including Dristan.

I stand, pulling the wrapped grimoire from my pocket. Simple black paper with a silver ribbon—appropriate for what it represents.

"I drew your name," I say unnecessarily, crossing to where she sits beside Dristan. "I spent three hours searching for this. Combed through half the antiquarian bookshops in Paris."

"Three hours?" Ivan mutters. "That long, huh?"

"Hush," Juliette elbows him.

I set the box in front of Cassandra, and she looks up at me with those eyes that are too knowing, too perceptive. She sees the burden I'm carrying. The apology I'm trying to make.

"Gavriil—" she starts.

"Open it first," I interrupt gently. "Then I'll explain."

Her hands are shaking slightly as she unties the ribbon. Pregnancy hormones, probably. Or maybe she knows this is more than just a gift.

The silk falls away, revealing a small leather-bound book. Ancient. Delicate. The kind of grimoire that costs a fortune and requires special permits just to purchase.

"Seventeenth century," I say as she lifts it carefully. "A treatise on resurrection magic. Theory, practice, ethics. Written by a French witch who spent her entire life studying the boundary between death and life."

Cassandra's breath catches. "Gavriil, this is—"

"Knowledge." I meet her eyes. "Agency. Choice. Everything I took from you when I forced that brand onto your skin."

The room goes completely still.

Across from me, Dristan's hands flatten on the table. I can see his knuckles turning white. See the ancient fury in his eyes rising to the surface like a shark scenting blood.

"You branded her," he says, voice deadly quiet, "because it served your political agenda. Forced a magical bond on her without consent. Kept me from reaching her for months while she suffered."

"Yes." I don't look away from him. Don't flinch. "I did."

"And now you think a book makes that right?"

"No." The word comes out firm. Final. "Nothing makes it right. Nothing can undo what I did or erase the cost." I turn back to Cassandra, making sure she hears this. Making sure they *all* hear it. "I branded you because my clan needed the alliance. Because the Ursa community was fracturing, and we needed the Deveraux power to survive. Because politically, strategically, it was the right move for my people."

"But?" Cassandra prompts softly.

"But it was wrong for you." I force the words out, each one a small surrender of the pride that's kept me alive this far. "It hurt you. Isolated you. Took away your choice and your freedom. And it tortured the man you love by keeping him away when you needed him most."

Dristan's chair scrapes back. He's standing now, all coiled vampire fury barely contained in civilized skin.

"Sit down," Cassandra says quietly.

"Cassie—"

"Dristan. Please. Sit down."

He does, but only because she asked. His eyes never leave mine, and the message in them is crystal clear: *You hurt her again, and I will end you. Alliance be damned.*

"I'm not asking for forgiveness," I continue, looking at Dristan now instead of Cassandra. "Not from you. You have every right to hate me. To want me dead. I took five months of your life with her. Five months you can never get back."

"No," he snaps, voice like broken glass. "You took *more* than that. And no—you can't give it back."

"But I can give her this." I gesture to the grimoire. "Knowledge about the magic that brought Luciana back. Understanding of the forces she wielded when she broke my brand using my grief as a conduit. The book can't undo what I did. But maybe it can help her understand what she's capable of. What she chose to do with the power I forced on her."

Cassandra's fingers trace the leather cover, and I see tears gathering in her eyes.

"The branding was necessary," I say, and I believe it. "My clan needed the alliance. Your family needed our strength. The supernatural world needed to see that bears and witches could unite. All of that is true."

"But?" Luciana prompts from beside me.

"But necessity doesn't erase harm." I look at Cassandra again. "You paid the price for that alliance with your freedom, your peace, your safety. You shouldn't have had to. And I'm sorry that you did."

"Gavriil—" Cassandra starts, but I hold up a hand.

"I'm not sorry I did it," I clarify, because I won't lie to her. Won't pretend I regret the choice that saved my clan and brought Luciana back. *I'm sorry it cost you so much.* I'm sorry I didn't find another way. And I'm sorry that the man you love had to watch you suffer and couldn't do anything to stop it."

Dristan's laugh is bitter. "Pretty words, Ursa King."

"Not pretty. True." I meet his ancient gaze. "You have every right to hate me. I would, in your position. But Cassandra asked us all here tonight. Asked us to choose each other despite the blood and betrayal and pain. So I'm trying." I gesture to the book. "This is me trying. Giving her knowledge. Choice. The things I took when I forced my magic into her skin."

The silence stretches, taut as a bowstring.

"Dristan."

Juliette's voice cuts through the tension like a blade —quiet, but carrying centuries of authority. The family elder. The Head Witch who gave her consent for the brand, as was tradition.

She rises from her seat, amethyst eyes fixed on the

millenary vampire who's been watching me all night with murder in his gaze.

"I approved the match," she says simply. "I gave my consent for the branding ceremony. As Cassandra's elder, as the matriarch of the Deveraux line, that was my right and my responsibility under our laws." She pauses, letting the weight of her words settle. "Which means the fault is also mine."

Dristan's eyes snap to her, something dangerous flickering in their depths.

"Gavriil acted to secure his clan," Juliette continues, her voice steady. "But I enabled it. I sanctioned it. I stood as witness when he bound her, knowing full well what it would cost." Her gaze doesn't waver. "You want someone to blame for the months you couldn't reach her? Blame me, too. I am as complicit in her suffering as he is."

"Juliette—" Ivan starts, but she silences him with a look.

"No." She turns back to Dristan. "I won't let Gavriil shoulder this alone. The branding followed our traditions, our laws, our way. I could have refused consent. I could have found another path for the alliance. But I didn't." Her voice softens, filling with regret. "I chose expediency over her happiness. Political stability over her freedom. I followed the same path of arranged matches our family had taken for centuries—a path I myself endured. And for that, I am sorry."

The silence that follows is profound.

Dristan stares at Juliette, and I see the war playing

out in his expression. The desire to hate us both. The recognition that she's right—that the fault is shared. That witch law gave us the framework, even if we chose to use it.

"You're the Head Witch," he says finally, voice low and dangerous. "You could have stopped it."

"Yes," Juliette agrees. "I could have. And I didn't. That is my shame to carry."

"So you both—" Dristan's hands flatten on the table again. "You both chose your politics over her pain."

"Yes," I say, because there's no point in denying it.

"Yes," Juliette echoes.

Dristan looks between us, and for a moment, I think he might actually attack. Might let a millennium of vampire fury loose in this room and damn the consequences.

But then Cassandra stands.

She's six months pregnant, glowing with violet magic and carrying the most powerful baby in supernatural history. And she looks at me with eyes that have seen too much pain but somehow still choose forgiveness.

"Baby—" Dristan's voice holds a warning.

She touches his shoulder, and I see the way he immediately settles under her hand. The way centuries of fury bank themselves because she asked him to.

That's love.

The kind I forced into being between us, but which exists naturally, purely, between them.

"I forgive you," Cassandra says, and the words land

like stones in still water. "*Both* of you. Not because what you did was right. Not because it didn't hurt. But because I understand why you did it. And because you're not pretending it didn't cost me everything."

"Cassandra—" I start, but she shakes her head.

"I forgive you because Luciana is alive. Because your brand gave me the power to bring her back. Because in the end, your magic—terrible as it was—saved someone." She glances at Luciana, who's watching with tears in her violet eyes. "That has to count for something."

"It doesn't erase what he did," Dristan says flatly.

"No." Cassandra's hand tightens on his shoulder. "It doesn't. And you don't have to forgive him. That's your choice. Your right. But I do. For myself. For our family. For the baby who's going to need all of us to protect them."

As if in agreement, her belly moves visibly. The baby kicking, responding to the magic and emotion swirling through the room.

Cassandra looks down at her stomach, then back at me, and smiles. "They agree with me, apparently. So thank you, Gavriil. For the book. For the apology. For being honest about all of it."

I nod, not trusting my voice.

Dristan hasn't moved. Hasn't softened. But he's not trying to kill me, which under the circumstances feels like a victory.

"We're family now," Cassandra says firmly, looking around the table at all of us. "Complicated, messy, probably dysfunctional family. But family. And that means we show up for each other. Even when it's hard. Even when forgiveness feels impossible. We try."

"Hear, hear," Luciana says softly, raising her glass.

Others echo the toast, but Dristan stays silent. His eyes meet mine across the table, and the message is clear.

"I'm here because she asked me to be. Because she forgave you. But I haven't. And I won't. Not for what you did to her. Not for what you did to us."

I nod slightly, accepting his terms.

It's more than I deserve.

Cassandra sits back down, the grimoire clutched to her chest, and Dristan's arm immediately goes around her. Protective. Possessive. Warning me that she might have forgiven, but he's still watching. Still ready to destroy me if I ever hurt her again.

Good.

She deserves that kind of love. The kind that doesn't forgive easily. The kind that remembers every wound and stands guard against the next one.

Luciana takes my hand as I sit, squeezing gently. "That was brave," she whispers.

"Or stupid."

She's smiling. "I'm proud of you."

Around us, the party resumes. Music plays softly from somewhere—Juliette's doing, probably. Laughter returns. Little Katya babbles happily in Anya's arms, reaching for the candle flames with fascinated silver eyes. Cassandra's magic flickers in response, keeping the flames safely out of reach.

But I don't miss the way Dristan watches me for the rest of the evening.

Or the way his hand never leaves Cassandra's shoulder.

I branded her out of necessity. Hurt her to save my clan.

And he will never forgive me for it.

Nor should he.

That's the cost of the choice I made.

But at least now, she has the grimoire. Knowledge. Agency.

The power to choose her own path.

The things I took from her.

The things I'm trying, however inadequately, to return.

12
NIK: EMBERS OF FATE

The party has moved to the parlor for dessert, but I can't breathe.

Too many people. Too much noise. Too much emotion still raw from Clarissa's gift, from the compass exchange with Kaisner, from holding my father's journal like it's made of salvation and damnation all at once.

I need space. Air. Silence.

"I'll be right back," I murmur to Samara, kissing her temple. She looks at me with those knowing eyes—my anchor, my salvation—but she nods. Lets me go. Trusts me to return.

I hope I deserve that trust.

The study is blessedly empty. Dark wood panels, leather chairs, the scent of old books and older magic. I sink into a chair by the cold fireplace, Father's journal still clutched in my hands.

"My little flame," he wrote. *"You're going to change everything for our family."*

I close my eyes, trying to steady my breathing. The dragon is restless tonight. Has been since Kaisner arrived. Since we shook hands like civilized creatures instead of letting our fire speak.

Twenty days until I can brand Samara. Twenty days until she's mine forever, bound by magic and choice. Twenty days until—

The study door bursts open.

The cold hearth beside me roars to life with sudden flames.

I jolt upright, ready to apologize for intruding, but the words die in my throat.

Because the man who storms through that door isn't Gavriil or Ivan or any of the guests currently eating dessert in the parlor.

It's Willem Draken.

In his late forties, perhaps. His golden blonde hair touched with silver at the temples, his face carved by years and power and something else—something dark that moves beneath his skin like living shadow.

He's beautiful. Terrifying. Ancient in a way that has nothing to do with years.

And he doesn't see me.

I freeze, my heart hammering. This is impossible. Willem Draken died centuries ago. But he's *here*, real as flesh and blood, radiating power that makes my dragon cower and rage simultaneously.

"Willem, please—"

Juliette appears in the doorway behind him. Not the Juliette I know—wise, youthful on the outside but weary in spirit. This is Juliette in her prime. Maybe late thirties. Still breathtaking, her red hair swept up, her emerald eyes bright with fury and fear.

They can't see me. I'm a ghost in their timeline. A witness to something that happened over three centuries ago.

"Please, what?" Willem's voice is cold. Precise. Nothing like the warm father I've heard about in stories—the man who danced with Juliette when they were young, who called his children by pet names, who built an empire on love before the curse destroyed him. "Please forgive him? Please understand? Please let our son challenge me without consequences?"

"He's one and twenty," Juliette says, and there's steel in her voice. "He saw what you did to those servants. *Saw* what you're becoming. He had every right to—"

"He had no right!" Willem's roar shakes the room, and dragon fire flickers in his eyes. Not the warm gold of controlled power. Molten. Unstable. Wrong. "I am the Dragon King. I am his father. He will show me respect, or he will learn what happens to those who challenge my authority."

"Your authority?" Juliette's laugh is bitter. "Is that what you call it now? Authority?"

I can't breathe. Can't move. I'm watching the Dragon King I've heard about in legends—the conqueror, the tyrant, the monster—and recognizing too much of myself in his fury.

"They were *traitors*," Willem snarls. "Spies. I uncovered evidence. Letters. Correspondence with our enemies. They were feeding information to rival clans, plotting against us from within our own walls."

"They were servants!" Juliette steps forward, fearless despite the power radiating off him. "Human nobles who served your house for generations, Willem. Their families pledged loyalty to the Draken line before you were born. And you—" Her voice breaks. "You *burned them alive* based on letters that could have been forged. That *were* forged, if you'd taken the time to verify—"

"I don't need verification!" The flames in the hearth roar higher. "I am the Dragon King. My judgment is law. My instincts have kept this family safe for decades. If I say they were traitors, they were traitors."

"And if you're wrong?" Juliette's voice drops to something deadly. "If you killed innocents because the curse has made you see enemies in every face? Made you see threats where there are none?"

"I am never wrong." But there's something in Willem's voice now. Doubt. Fear. Quickly buried beneath rage. "They were planning to poison our stores. To assassinate Jan during the winter hunt. To—"

"Prove it." Juliette crosses her arms. "Show me this evidence. Let me examine these letters with my own magic. Let me verify—"

"I burned the evidence," Willem says flatly. "After

the execution. It was... contaminated. Dark magic. Dangerous to keep."

The silence that follows is damning.

"You burned the evidence," Juliette repeats slowly. "The only proof that three people deserved to die. Gone." She pauses. "Convenient."

"It was necessary—"

"It was murder!" Her voice cracks. "And you know it. You killed them because you *suspected* betrayal. Because your dragon whispered fear in your ear, and you listened. Because the curse has made you incapable of trusting anyone—even me."

I watch Willem's face. Watch the war playing out across his features. For a moment—just a moment—I see genuine uncertainty. The possibility that he was wrong. That the curse twisted his perception.

Then his expression hardens.

"Better to kill a potential traitor than risk my family," he says. "Better to act on suspicion than wait for certainty and lose everything. That is what a king does. That is what *survival* requires in this world."

And gods help me, I understand.

I understand the logic. The fear. The weight of responsibility that makes you see threats everywhere. That makes mercy feel like weakness and hesitation like death.

Because I've made similar calculations. Similar choices. Justified similar actions in the name of protecting what I love.

"Everyone knows the man I married is gone," Juliette whispers. "Everyone knows you've been consumed by the same curse that took your father. Your grandfather."

"There is no curse!" But even as Willem says it, he's pulling at his collar. Loosening his cravat. And I see them.

Death marks.

Black script crawling up his neck. Across his collarbone. Disappearing beneath his shirt where I know—I *know*—there are more. Names. Hundreds of names. Written in the ancient dragon language, each one a life claimed by dark magic.

Just like the marks on my chest.

"No curse?" Juliette's voice is deadly quiet. She crosses to him, and I see the moment she notices the new marks. The way her face goes pale. "Then what do you call that? What do you call the darkness that's been consuming you for five years? The way you wake screaming in languages that haven't been spoken in millennia?"

"Power." Willem's hand goes to his chest, covering the marks possessively. "I call it power. The magic that will ensure our family rules for generations. That will make the Draken name immortal."

"At what cost?" Juliette's reaching for him now, desperate. Her hand cups the side of his face—tender, pleading, the gesture of a woman trying to reach the man she married through the monster he's becoming. "Willem, please. I've been researching. I've found texts about the curse. Ways to break it. If we act now, before it takes you completely—"

"I don't need saving." He catches her wrist, and I see her flinch. See the way dragon fire flickers across his skin, hot enough to burn. "I need your support. Your magic. Your willingness to stand beside me instead of questioning every decision I make."

"I've stood beside you for twenty-six years." Tears are streaming down Juliette's face now. "I've borne your children. Built our legacy. Defended your rule. But I won't stand beside you while you become the monster your father was. While you destroy everything we built together."

"Then stand aside." Willem releases her wrist, and she stumbles back. "Stand aside and watch me build something greater than you could ever imagine."

"Father—"

A young man appears in the doorway. One and twenty, Juliette said. He's tall, golden-haired, with Willem's strong features and Juliette's eyes. Jan. The eldest son. A dragon shifter.

And he's staring at his father with a mixture of horror and defiance.

"Jan, go," Juliette says immediately. "Please. Go to your siblings. Keep them safe."

"No." Jan steps into the room, and I see dragon fire flicker in his eyes. Young. Untested. But brave. "I won't let him hurt you."

Willem laughs. It's a jarring sound. "Hurt her? She's my mate. My queen. I would never—"

"You just burned her." Jan gestures to Juliette's wrist, where angry red welts are already forming. "You hurt her every day with what you're becoming."

"What I'm becoming?" Willem turns on his son, and the temperature in the room skyrockets. "I'm becoming the greatest Dragon King in history. I'm becoming powerful enough to protect this family from any threat. To ensure our bloodline rules for centuries."

"You're becoming a murderer!" Jan's dragon rises to meet his father's challenge. Gold eyes blazing. Young fire sparking at his fingertips. "Those servants weren't traitors. You killed them because you see traitors *every-where*. Because the curse—"

He doesn't see Willem move.

None of us do.

One moment, Willem is across the room. The next, he has Jan by the throat, lifted off the ground, dragon scales rippling across his skin as his control shatters.

"You dare?" Willem's voice is barely human. Barely sane. "You dare challenge me? Question my judgment? I am the Dragon King. I have conquered nations. Destroyed armies. I have *earned* my throne through blood and fire and decades of sacrifice. And you—my whelp of a son—think you can stand in judgment of me?"

"Willem, stop!" Juliette's bleeding magic now. Violet light crackling through the air. "Put him down. Please. He's our boy. He's—"

"He's a traitor." Willem doesn't even look at her. His eyes are locked on Jan, who's struggling to breathe, clawing at his father's iron grip. "Just like those servants. Just like everyone who questions me. And traitors burn."

Fire erupts.

Not the controlled flame of a master. Wild. Vicious. Consuming.

Jan screams.

Juliette screams louder.

And I—

I can't move. Can't breathe. Can't do anything but watch as the Dragon King nearly kills his own son for daring to question his judgment. For daring to suggest he might be wrong.

Was Willem right about the servants? Were they truly traitors?

Or was it paranoia? The curse twisting his perceptions?

I'll never know. None of us will.

And that's the horror of it.

At the last moment—the very last moment before it's too late—Willem drops Jan.

The boy crumples to the floor, clothes singed, skin blistered, sobbing in pain and terror.

But even as he falls, I see it happening. Dragon healing. Faster than human, faster even than most supernatural creatures. The angry red burns already fading to pink. Blisters smoothing. Charred skin knitting itself back together with preternatural speed.

Then it hits me.

Dragons don't burn. Not permanently.

Willem knew that. Counted on it. Used pain as punishment, knowing it would leave no lasting scars on his son's flesh.

Only in his soul.

"Get out," Willem says, his voice dead. Empty. "Both of you. Get out of my sight before I finish what I started."

Juliette doesn't hesitate. She's there, pulling Jan up, supporting his weight. The burns are already half-healed, but Jan is still shaking. Still sobbing. Not from physical pain now, but from the knowledge that his father—his *father*—just tried to teach him obedience through fire.

"This isn't over," she says, and there's a promise in her voice. A vow. "I will find a way to save you, Willem. Even if I have to destroy the monster you've become to find the man I married."

"The man you married is dead." Willem turns away from them, staring into the roaring fireplace. At the flames that burn with his fury. "There is only the Dragon King now. Only power. Only the throne."

He touches his chest, and I see the death marks pulse. See the way they writhe and shift like living things.

"Only the curse," Juliette whispers. "May the gods have mercy on your soul."

She pulls Jan from the room, leaving Willem alone.

Leaving *me* alone with him.

He stands there for a long moment, staring at the

flames. Then his hand moves to his jacket. Pulls out a book.

A grimoire.

Black leather. Dragons engraved on the cover. Ancient runes. Pulsing with dark magic that makes my stomach turn.

The same grimoire Samara stole from Juliette's desk. The same grimoire I've been using for months. The same grimoire that's covering my chest with death marks identical to Willem's.

"Just one more," Willem whispers to the book. To himself. To the curse consuming him. "Just one more name. One more spell. One more piece of power, and I'll have enough. Enough to secure the throne. Enough to make them all bow. Enough to prove I was right. That they were traitors. That everything I did was necessary."

He stops.

His hand goes to his chest, where the marks are spreading.

"They were traitors," he says again, but his voice cracks. Doubt bleeding through. "They had to be. I wouldn't have... I couldn't have killed innocents. Not for nothing. Not because of unfounded suspicion."

For just a moment, I see the man beneath the monster. The father who loved his children. Who built an empire with Juliette by his side. Who's terrified that everything he's done—every life he's taken—might have been for nothing.

"Juliette," he whispers. "Gods. What if I was wrong?"

But then the grimoire pulses, and his expression goes cold again. Dead again.

"I wasn't wrong," he says firmly. "I'm never wrong. I'm the Dragon King. My judgment is law."

He opens the grimoire, and I see dark magic swirl around him like smoke.

"And if I must become a monster to protect my family," he says, "then so be it."

Then his eyes lift from the page.

And meet mine.

For one impossible, horrifying moment, Willem Draken *sees* me. Across three centuries. Across death and time and the veil between past and present.

His golden eyes—molten with dragon fire and death magic—lock onto mine.

And he smiles.

Not cruel. Not mocking.

Understanding.

You see it now, don't you? his expression seems to say. *You see how easy it is. How necessary. How the line between protection and monstrosity is so thin you don't even notice when you cross it.*

"Embers of fate," he whispers, and I realize with dawning horror that he's not speaking to his son.

He's speaking to *me*.

Across time. Across death. The Dragon King to his successor.

"The throne demands sacrifice," Willem says, his voice echoing strangely. Present and past blurring. "The curse demands blood."

He steps closer, and my breath catches.

He can see me. Truly see me.

How—?

Then, I remember. Willem Von Draken wasn't just the first Dragon King in my lineage. He was a seer. One of the most powerful in history. Able to see threads of fate, glimpses of futures yet to come. A gift Clarissa inherited.

He's not only seeing me as I am now—a ghost watching from the present.

He's seeing me as I will be. As I'm destined to become.

The next Dragon King. The next victim of the curse.

"Beware, young dragon—" His smile turns cold. Empty. "The greatest threat to your crown won't come from enemies outside your walls."

His hand reaches out—impossibly, across centuries —and the ghost of his touch settles against my chest. Right where my own death marks hide beneath my shirt. His fingers rest there, and the marks burn as if they recognize their creator.

"It will come from the one who shares your blood," Willem continues, his seer's eyes looking *through* me, seeing futures I can't imagine. "The one who wants what you have. The one who smiles while sharpening their blade."

The scene fractures.

Reality splinters like broken glass.

And I'm falling—

—gasping—

—back into the present.

I'm still in the study. Still in the chair. Father's journal has fallen from my hands, pages scattered across the floor.

The hearth is cold again. Dark. As if the flames never existed.

But I'm not alone anymore.

"Nik?"

NIK: A DRAGON'S CURSE

"Nik?"

Samara's in the doorway, worry etched across her beautiful face. "You've been gone for twenty minutes. Are you—" She stops. Sees whatever expression is on my face. "What happened?"

I can't answer.

Can't tell her that I just watched my future play out three centuries ago.

Can't explain that Willem Draken—the monster, the tyrant, the Dragon King who fell to the curse—used the same grimoire I've been using. Made the same choices I'm making. Justified the same darkness in the name of power and protection.

And I still don't know whether he was right.

If those servants were truly traitors or if the curse made him see enemies where there were none.

That's the terror of it. The uncertainty. The knowledge that every decision I make could be correct—or catastrophically wrong—and I might never know the difference.

My hand goes to my chest. To where the death marks hide beneath my shirt. Ten new names since Scotland. The last three appeared just hours ago—accidental, uncontrolled, during a moment when my guard was down, and my dragon surged. Three more lives claimed by dragon magic and ambition.

Were they all necessary? Or has the curse already twisted my judgment?

Magic that's transforming me into the very thing I swore I'd never become.

"Nik." Samara crosses to me, kneeling in front of the chair. Her hands find mine. Warm. Real. Anchoring me to the present. "Talk to me. Please."

"I saw him," I manage. "Willem. Here. In this study."

She doesn't question it. Doesn't doubt. She knows about the temporal warps that have been happening in Deveraux Manor. Knows that magic and history bleed together in these old walls.

"What did you see?" she asks quietly.

Everything. The argument. The burns. The grimoire. The curse consuming him piece by piece until nothing human remained.

The uncertainty. The paranoia. The inability to know if his actions were protection or madness.

"The end," I whisper. "I saw what happens when a Dragon King chooses power over love. When he lets the curse take him. When he can no longer tell the difference between threats and shadows."

Samara's breath catches. "Nik—"

"I'm becoming him." The confession tears out of me. "The grimoire. The death marks. The way my dragon is getting harder to control. The way I justify every spell, every curse, every life taken in the name of securing the throne." I meet her eyes, and I see my terror reflected there. "What if I'm already wrong? What if the choices I've made—the people I've hurt—weren't necessary? What if it's just the curse making me believe I'm protecting us when I'm really destroying everything?"

She stares at me, and I see horror dawn in her eyes.

"But you said you were done with the grimoire," she whispers. "You promised after Scotland you'd stop. That we'd find another way."

My hand goes to my chest instinctively, to where the marks hide beneath my shirt—and beneath layers of carefully maintained glamour.

"I will." The lie catches in my throat. "I'll... try to."

"Wait—" She stops, reading something in my expression. Her eyes drop to where my hand presses against my chest. "Nik. Are there more?"

I can't do this. Can't watch her face when she sees.

But I owe her the truth.

"Yes."

The word hangs between us like a death sentence.

"How many?" Her voice is barely audible.

"I don't know anymore." I force my hand away from my chest. "I've been hiding them. Glamour. It works for a while, but the curse scripture is magic-resistant. It bleeds through eventually. I have to recast it every few hours."

"Show me."

"Sam—"

"Show me." Steel now, beneath the hurt. "If you've been hiding this from me—if you've been lying to me every time we—" She stops, horror dawning. "Every time I touched you. Every time we were together. You were hiding them."

Shame burns through me like dragon fire.

"I didn't want you to see," I admit quietly. "Didn't want you to know how bad it's gotten."

"Show. Me."

I close my eyes. Drop the glamour.

The magic peels away like burning skin, and I feel the curse marks blaze across my chest—hot, angry, undeniable. When I open my eyes, I force myself to look down.

The dragon tattoo—my clan's sigil—is barely visible anymore beneath the writhing mass of names. They cover my chest, my ribs, crawling down toward my stomach. Dark ink that seems to pulse with its own malevolent life.

Ancient dragon script.

Dozens of them.

Maybe more.

Samara's breath catches, sharp and painful.

"Nik," she whispers. "Oh gods, Nik."

I can't look at her. Can't bear to see the horror, the betrayal, the realization of what I've become.

"How long?" she asks. "How long have you been hiding this?"

"Weeks." The confession tears out of me. "Since before Scotland. The glamour gets harder to maintain each time. The curse fights it. Burns through faster."

"And you said nothing." Her voice breaks. "You looked me in the eye. You touched me. You let me believe—"

"I know."

Silence.

Then: "Take off your shirt."

"What?"

"All of it." Her voice is cold now, clinical. "I want to see everything you've been hiding from me."

I reach for the buttons of my shirt with hands that aren't quite steady.

"Wait." Samara's voice stops me. She crosses the room, closes the study door. Locks it. "I don't want anyone seeing this."

The click of the lock sounds like a cell door closing.

I unbutton my shirt, fingers working down each button slowly, deliberately. The fabric slides from my shoulders, exposing every inch of cursed skin to the light. To her gaze.

The silence stretches.

I force myself to stand still. To let her look. To not cover myself like the coward I am.

"Turn around," she says finally.

I do.

I hear her sharp intake of breath behind me.

"Your back," she whispers. "Nik, they're on your back now."

"I know."

"How far?"

"Down to my waist." I close my eyes. "They started appearing there two weeks ago."

Footsteps. Then her hand on my shoulder blade, tracing the script I can't see but feel burning every moment of every day. Her touch is soothing, healing in a way I don't think she even suspects. Even now—even furious, even betrayed—her magic reaches for mine instinctively. Light trying to soothe darkness.

I don't deserve it.

"There are so many," she breathes. "How many people have you—"

"I don't know." The words come out harsh. "I stopped counting. Stopped trying to justify it. Every time the dragon gets too volatile, every time I feel like I'm losing control, I use the grimoire. And every time, another name appears."

Her hand drops away.

"Face me."

I turn back around.

Samara stands there, arms wrapped around herself, staring at my chest like it's a crime scene. Her eyes track each name, each line of script, the way they overlap and weave together into a tapestry of my damnation.

"The dragon tattoo is almost gone," she says

distantly. "Your clan's sigil. Your heritage. It's being consumed by the curse."

"I know."

"And you kept using the grimoire anyway."

"Yes."

"Why?" The word explodes from her. "After everything, after all your promises—why?"

"Because I need the power!" The confession rips out of me, raw and desperate. "Every spell brings me closer to the throne. Every name makes me stronger. Strong enough to unite the dragon clans. Strong enough to—"

"To beat Kaisner," she finishes, and there's horror in her voice now. "This is about him. About your rivalry."

"It's about more than that." I'm pacing now, heat radiating off me in waves. "At first, yes—I wanted the throne to protect our kind. To unite the scattered clans under one banner. Give dragons a future instead of endless territorial wars." My hands clench into fists. "That was real. That mattered."

"And now?"

"Now?" I laugh, bitter and broken. "Now there's something else. Something dark rushing through my veins like poison ever since Kaisner revealed himself. This need—this hunger—to prove I'm stronger. Better. More worthy of the crown."

I turn to face her, and I know she can see it. The darkness bleeding through my control. The corruption taking root.

"I can't stop, Sam. Because every time I use the grimoire, I get one step closer. One spell closer to having enough power to challenge him. To take what's mine by right."

"What's yours by right?" She stares at me like I'm a stranger. "Nik, you sound—"

"Obsessed?" I finish for her. "Consumed? Yes. I know. I feel it eating away at everything I was. Everything I wanted to be." My voice drops to a whisper. "I'm terrified, Samara. Terrified of losing. Of Kaisner taking the throne. Of everything I've sacrificed—everyone I've damned—being for nothing."

"So you keep using it," she says slowly. "Keep binding more souls. Keep letting the curse consume you. Because you'd rather become a monster than lose to Kaisner."

I want to deny it. To justify it. To tell her she doesn't understand.

But the words stick in my throat.

"I don't know anymore," I admit quietly.

"Then stop."

"I can't." The confession breaks something in me. "Sam, I've tried. Every time I swear it's the last spell, the darkness whispers that I'm so close. One more name. One more push. And I listen because—" I stop. Force the truth out. "Because I'm terrified that without the grimoire, I'm not strong enough. That everything I've sacrificed will be for nothing."

"So you'd rather become what you hate than admit you might be wrong?"

The question hangs between us.

Would I?

"I don't know how to stop," I whisper. "The obsession—it's in my blood now. Part of me. And I'm scared that without the grimoire, I'm just another cursed dragon with delusions of grandeur."

"And with it?" Her voice is cold now. "What are you with it, Nikolaas?"

I look down at my chest. At the countless names consuming my clan's sigil. At the proof of everything I've become.

"Damned," I whisper. "With or without the throne, I'm already damned."

The confession settles over us like ash. I watch her absorb it—the finality of it. That I know what I'm becoming, and I can't stop anyway.

Silence stretches between us, heavy and devastating.

"Baby," I breathe. "I'm so sorry."

"Sorry?" Her voice rises. "You're sorry? Nik, you're *dying*. The curse is eating you alive, and instead of telling me—instead of letting me help—you've been lying to my face every single day."

"What could you have done?" The question comes out harsher than I intend. "What could anyone do? The curse is unstoppable. Every dragon who's tried to break it has failed."

"So you just gave up?" She's shaking now. "You decided to handle it alone, consequences be damned?"

"I'm trying to protect you—"

"By lying? By hiding?" She gestures at my chest, at the writhing mass of names. "This isn't protection,

Nikolaas. This is you drowning and refusing to reach for the lifeline."

"There is no lifeline!" The words explode from me, and with them, heat. The study temperature spikes. "Don't you understand? The curse doesn't end. It just gets worse. More names. More death. Until there's nothing left of me but scripture and fire."

"Then we find another way," she says fiercely. "We ask Cassandra. We consult with Clarissa's coven. We search for answers together. But we don't—" Her voice breaks. "We don't lie to each other. We don't hide in the dark and pretend everything's fine."

"I didn't know how to tell you." The admission feels like ripping out my own heart. "Every time I tried, I'd look at you and see how much you already carry. How much you sacrifice to be with me. How tired you are. And I couldn't—" I stop. Breathe. "I couldn't bear adding this to your burden."

"My burden?" She stares at me like I'm a stranger. "Nik, I'm your mate. Your partner. Carrying your burdens is what love means. But you have to let me in. You *have* to trust me with the truth."

"I do trust you—"

"Then why have you been lying for weeks?" She takes a step back. "Why am I only seeing this now because I cornered you at a Christmas party?"

I have no answer for that.

"Twenty days," Samara says, and there are tears in her eyes now. "Twenty days until you can brand me. Make me yours..." She cups my face, forcing me to look at her. "But will it be Nikolaas Draken who brands me? The man I love? Or will it be the Dragon King? The monster the curse is making you?"

I want to tell her it'll be me. That I'm strong enough to resist. That love is enough to break the curse.

But moments ago, I saw the future. Saw what happens to dragon kings who believe they can control the darkness. Who justify every atrocity in the name of protection.

"I don't know," I admit. And the truth of it breaks something inside me. "I don't know, Sam. And that terrifies me."

She kisses me then. Desperate. Claiming. Trying to anchor me to humanity through touch alone.

"Then we have twenty days," she whispers against my lips. "Twenty days to save you. To find another way. To break the curse before it breaks you."

"And if we can't?"

She pulls back, and I see determination burning in her eyes. The same determination that helped her survive being the Ursa Princess in a clan of ruthless bears. The same strength that made her choose me despite every warning.

"Then I'll do what Juliette should have done," she says. "Save you even if it means losing you."

"Sam—"

"I won't watch you become him, Nik." Her voice is steel. "I won't stand by while the curse takes you. Even if it means you hate me. Even if—"

I kiss her again. Silencing her. Thanking her. Terrified of her.

Because I know she means it.

And I know that in twenty days, one of us is going to break.

Either I'll master the curse and brand her, securing the throne and our future together.

Or she'll save me by destroying everything I've worked for.

There is no middle ground.

There is no safe path.

There is only fire and darkness and the ghost of Willem Draken's fate haunting every choice I make.

And the terrible knowledge that I might already be the monster.

That I might have already crossed the line.

That those names on my chest might be innocents I killed because the curse whispered paranoia in my ear.

Just like Willem.

14

CASSANDRA: THE UNRAVELING

Something's wrong with Nikolaas.

I notice it the moment he and Samara return to the parlor. The way his ice-blue eyes scan the room like he's cataloging threats. The way his jaw is clenched so tight, I can see the muscle jumping. The way his hand keeps going to his chest, as if checking for something hidden beneath his shirt.

Samara's knuckles are white where she grips his hand, and her expression—gods, her expression terrifies me. Like she's watching a bomb and doesn't know when it'll detonate.

"Everything alright?" I ask as they settle back onto the sofa.

"Fine," Nikolaas says, but his voice is too tight. Too controlled.

Samara says nothing. Just keeps holding his hand like it's the only thing keeping him tethered to earth.

Around us, the party continues. Dristan pours

wine for Juliette. Ivan makes another sardonic comment that has Vlad laughing. Katya creates tiny snowflakes that melt on her mother's nose. Luciana and Gavriil are deep in quiet conversation, his hand resting on hers like he's afraid she might disappear.

It should be perfect.

It *was* perfect.

But now there's a wrongness in the air. A tension that makes my magic flicker at the edges of my vision. The baby kicks hard, responding to my anxiety, and I have to take a breath to steady myself.

"More wine?" I offer brightly, trying to recapture the warmth from earlier. "Or coffee? Ivan brought some ridiculously expensive blend that he claims will change my life."

"It will," Ivan confirms. "I don't make false promises about coffee."

"Just about everything else," Dristan mutters, but he's smiling.

The moment should be light. Easy. But I can feel it —the way Nikolaas' eyes keep finding Kaisner across the room. The way his dragon is too close to the surface, making the temperature rise incrementally.

Kaisner notices. Of course he does. He's a dragon too, and they're always aware of each other. Always measuring, assessing, calculating dominance.

"Nikolaas," Kaisner says carefully, his maroon eyes steady. "Are you—"

"I'm fine." But Nikolaas' hand goes to his chest

again, and something flickers in his expression. Fear. Suspicion. Something that makes my stomach drop.

Clarissa shifts beside Kaisner, her seer's eyes going distant for just a moment. Then they snap back to the present, and she looks at her brother with barely concealed alarm.

"Nik," she says quietly. "Maybe you should—"

"I said I'm fine." His voice is sharp now. Cutting. "Why does everyone keep asking me that?"

"Maybe it's because you look like you're about to explode," Ivan observes with typical bluntness. "And while I appreciate drama as much as the next person, perhaps we could avoid bloodshed at Cassandra's Christmas party?"

"Ivan," Juliette warns.

But Nikolaas is standing now, and the temperature in the room spikes. Dragon fire sparks in his eyes— gold overwhelming the ice-blue. Unstable. Wrong.

"You want to talk about bloodshed?" Nikolaas' voice is low. Dangerous. "You want to talk about threats and enemies and who we should trust?"

"Nik, sit down," Samara pleads, tugging at his hand. "Please. Whatever you saw in that study—"

"What I saw was the truth." He pulls his hand from hers, and I see her flinch. "I saw what happens when you trust the wrong people. When you welcome traitors into your home like they're family."

The room goes silent.

"Traitors?" Kaisner stands slowly, carefully. His

dragon rising to meet the challenge whether he wants it to or not. "What are you talking about?"

"You know exactly what I'm talking about." Nikolaas's hands are clenched into fists, and I can see dragon scales starting to ripple across his knuckles. "You've wanted the throne since the moment you realized you had dragon blood and might have a claim."

"Nik, stop," Clarissa says, moving between them. "This isn't the time for—whatever you think is happening isn't—"

"Isn't what?" Nikolaas' laugh is bitter. "Isn't real? Isn't a threat? Tell me, Clarissa—do your visions show him striking tonight? Tomorrow?"

"My visions show you making a terrible mistake," Clarissa says, and there are tears in her eyes. "Right now. If you don't stop this."

But Nikolaas isn't listening. His focus is locked on Kaisner with an intensity that makes my skin crawl.

"We shook hands tonight," Nikolaas says. "We pretended to be civil. To be family. But I know what you are. What you want."

"What I want," Kaisner says carefully, his maroon eyes steady despite the threat radiating from Nikolaas, "is to not fight you in Cassandra's parlor. What I want is for Clarissa to not have to choose between her brother and her mate. What I want—"

"Is my throne." Nikolaas takes a step forward, and dragon fire crackles at his fingertips. "You want my clan. You want the crown. You want my mate... You want everything I've worked for, everything I've sacrificed—"

"Nikolaas!" Samara's voice cracks. "He doesn't—Kaisner has never—"

"He wants what I have," Nikolaas snarls, and I see something wild in his eyes. Something that looks like fear wrapped in fury. "He smiles while sharpening his blade. He waits for the perfect moment to—" He stops. Blinks. Like he's hearing his words for the first time. But the damage is done.

"Sharpening my blade?" Kaisner's voice is deadly quiet now. His dragon rising, not in challenge but in defense. "Nikolaas, I've been open about our rivalry from the beginning. I've never kept secret my ambition to sit on the Dragon King throne. I've never plotted. Never schemed. Never waited to stab you in the back." His maroon eyes narrow. "If you can't tell the difference between an honest rival and a traitor—if the curse has progressed that far—then maybe we do have a problem."

"Don't talk about the curse," Nikolaas warns.

"Why not?" Kaisner's control is fraying now, too. "It's killing you. Everyone can see it. The way you can't trust anyone anymore. The way you see enemies in every shadow. The way you're looking at me right now like I'm the monster when you're the one—"

Dragon fire erupts.

Not directed at anyone. Just—out. Wild. Uncontrolled. Nikolaas's power exploding in response to rage and fear and whatever he saw in that study.

The curtains catch fire instantly.

"Nik!" Samara throws her magic at the flames, winter ice battling dragon heat.

But Nikolaas isn't stopping. He's advancing on Kaisner, and Kaisner—gods, Kaisner can't back down. Not without losing face. Not without admitting weakness.

"That's enough!" Gavriil's voice booms across the room, and suddenly, there's a bear shifter between the two dragons. Alpha. Dominant. Radiating enough power to make even dragons pause. "Both of you. Stand. Down."

"This doesn't concern you, Ursa King," Nikolaas says, but at least he's not throwing more fire.

"It concerns me when you're burning down Cassandra's house," Gavriil replies. "It concerns me when my sister is trying to hold together a man who's falling apart. It concerns me when—"

"When what?" Ivan's voice cuts in, sharp and sardonic. "When you suddenly care about consequences? About forcing bonds on people? About torture disguised as tradition?"

Oh no.

"Ivan, don't," Juliette warns.

But Ivan's standing now too, and there's something dark in his expression. Something that's been simmering since the gift exchange. Since Gavriil's apology that Dristan still hasn't accepted.

"You branded Cassandra," Ivan says, his voice carrying that particular vampire coldness. "You tortured Dristan by keeping him from his mate. You justified it with politics and tradition and necessity. And now you want to lecture dragons about control?"

"That's different," Gavriil growls.

"Is it?" Ivan takes a step forward. "Because from where I'm standing, you're just as much a monster as Nikolaas is becoming. The only difference is you're better at hiding behind words like 'duty' and 'clan.'"

"Ivan." Dristan's voice holds a warning, but there's approval in his eyes. Because he hasn't forgiven Gavriil either. Because he's been waiting for someone to say it.

"You want to talk about monsters?" Gavriil's bear is surfacing now, silver eyes flashing. "You—a vampire who's lived for centuries on human blood. Who's killed more people than you can count. Your kind murdered my father, so forgive me if I don't trust your moral judgment—"

"My *kind*?" Ivan's voice goes deadly quiet. "You're going to judge me based on what another vampire did to your father? That's convenient, Gavriil. Blame an entire species for one creature's actions while defending your own 'necessary' torture." His eyes flash. "Yes, let's talk about blood and choices and consent. Let's talk about how you forced a magical bond on a pregnant witch to secure your political alliance."

"It was necessary!" Gavriil roars.

"It was torture!" Ivan roars back.

And suddenly everyone's standing. Everyone's shouting. Taking sides.

Vlad moves to Gavriil's side—pack loyalty, brother before stranger.

Dristan moves to Ivan's—maker and fledgling, three centuries of bond.

Luciana's trying to hold Gavriil back while Juliette does the same with Ivan.

Clarissa stands between two dragons—her brother and her mate—magic crackling as she tries to separate them.

Samara's pulling at Nikolaas, desperate and terrified.

Anya's holding Katya close, the toddler starting to cry from all the shouting and magic and anger saturating the air.

And I—

I can't do this.

I can't watch my family tear itself apart.

I can't be the reason they're all here, the reason they're fighting, the reason everything's falling apart.

"STOP IT!" I scream, but my voice is lost in the chaos.

Dristan says something cutting to Gavriil about penance.

Gavriil responds with something about vampire superiority.

Nikolaas is still advancing on Kaisner despite Samara's attempts to stop him.

Ivan makes another sardonic comment that only makes everything worse.

Pain lances through my belly as the baby kicks violently, and I gasp, one hand flying to my stomach.

My magic flares violet, responding to my distress.

And I can't—

I can't—

I run.

Through the parlor. Down the hall. Out onto the balcony, where the night air is cold and clean and blessedly quiet.

The door slams shut behind me, muffling the shouting, and I collapse against the railing.

Sobbing.

I just wanted one night.

One perfect Christmas in May, where my chosen family could celebrate being together. Where we could exchange gifts and laugh and remember that for all the blood and betrayal and impossible circumstances—we chose each other.

But instead, they're tearing everything apart.

And it's my fault.

I invited them. I pushed them together. I insisted we could be family despite every reason we shouldn't be.

The baby kicks again, and I press my hand to my belly.

"I'm sorry," I whisper. "I'm so sorry. I wanted to give you a family. A real family. Not just me and your father, but aunts and uncles and cousins who would love you. Who would protect you. Who would choose you even when it was hard."

But maybe that was naive.

Some wounds run too deep to heal.

Forced bonds and old resentments and supernatural politics might be too much for even love to overcome.

15

CASSANDRA: SNOW AND FORGIVENESS

"Cassandra."

I jolt, spinning to find Dristan in the doorway. Not angry. Not cold. Just—concerned.

"They were fighting," I manage through tears.

"Yes."

"I ruined everything."

"No." He crosses to me, and his hands settle on my shoulders. Gentle. Grounding. "You tried to build something beautiful. They're the ones who couldn't hold it together for one night."

"But I should have known. Should have realized that putting Nikolaas and Kaisner together—that having Gavriil and you in the same room—that asking Ivan to—"

"You shouldn't have to manage everyone's issues," Dristan interrupts. "You shouldn't have to be the glue holding everyone together. You're six months pregnant, and you've been through hell. The fact that you even tried to give us this gift—" His voice cracks slightly. "That's extraordinary."

"It doesn't feel extraordinary," I sob. "It feels like a disaster."

"Most extraordinary things do," he says quietly. "Come back inside. Please. You need to see what they've done."

"I can't. I can't watch them—"

"They've stopped," Dristan says. "Or they're stopping. I can't quite tell. But there's a lot of snow inside suddenly, and everyone looks very guilty."

Despite everything, I laugh. It's watery and broken, but it's a laugh.

"Snow?"

"Katya, I think. She started crying, and her magic responded. Now the entire parlor looks like a winter wonderland, and everyone's standing around looking ashamed of themselves."

I take a shaky breath. Then another. My magic settles slowly, the violet flickering fading back to normal levels.

"Are they hurt?"

"Only their pride." Dristan offers me his hand. "Come. Let them apologize. Let them remember why they came here tonight."

I take his hand, and together we walk back inside.

The parlor is indeed covered in snow.

Thick, heavy drifts piled in corners. Delicate flakes still falling from the ceiling where Katya's magic continues to pour out in response to her distress. The fire in the hearth is out, extinguished by ice. The curtains that Nikolaas lit are damp and smoking but no longer burning.

And everyone—every single person—is standing in guilty silence.

Nikolaas and Kaisner are on opposite sides of the room now, both looking shaken and ashamed.

Gavriil and Ivan are no longer shouting, though they're pointedly not looking at each other.

Samara's face is streaked with tears.

Clarissa looks devastated.

Anya's rocking Katya, the toddler hiccupping through the last of her tears.

And they all turn to look at me when I enter.

"Cassandra—" Gavriil starts.

"I'm sorry—" Nikolaas says at the same time.

"We didn't mean—" Ivan begins.

I hold up a hand, and they all fall silent.

For a long moment, I just look at them. At my impossible, complicated, absolutely chaotic family.

Ivan's impeccable hair is frosted with Katya's snow. The Christmas tree is somehow half frozen, half singed. Gavriil is still in Ursa King mode, soot on his stern face, standing between two full-grown dragons. And we're all dressed for a party.

Then I start to laugh.

It bubbles up from somewhere deep, slightly hysterical, definitely tinged with tears. But it's real.

"Look at us," I say, gesturing at the snow-covered

parlor. At the burned curtains and melted decorations. At the guilty faces and separated sides. "Fighting at a Christmas party in May because one pregnant witch wanted to celebrate family. We're ridiculous."

"We're sorry," Samara says, and she sounds wrecked. "Cassie, we're so sorry. Nik didn't mean—he saw something in the study, something that—"

"I know," I say quietly. Looking at Nikolaas, who can't quite meet my eyes. "I know about the temporal warps. About Willem. About the curse." I take a breath. "And I know that sometimes the past bleeds into the present and makes us see threats that might not be real."

Nikolaas flinches as if I've struck him.

"But here's the thing," I continue, moving to the center of the room. Standing in the snow that a toddler created to cool everyone's tempers. "We don't get to choose our lineage. Nikolaas doesn't get to choose the curse. Gavriil doesn't get to undo the branding. Dristan doesn't get to forget five months of torture. Ivan doesn't get to erase his resentment."

I turn slowly, making sure I meet every eye.

"But we do get to choose what we do with it. We get to choose whether we let our past destroy us or whether we build something new from the ashes. We get to choose family—messy, imperfect, absolutely chaotic family—or we get to choose isolation."

The baby kicks, and I press my hand to my belly.

"This little one is going to be born into our dysfunction," I say. "They're going to grow up knowing that Uncle Nikolaas struggles with a curse. That Uncle Gavriil made terrible choices. That Uncle Ivan is sarcastic to cover his pain. That their father was kept from their mother for months by politics and magic."

I look at each of them in turn.

"And you know what? That's okay. Because they're also going to know that we chose each other anyway. That we showed up. That we fought and forgave and kept trying even when it was impossibly hard."

Silence.

Then Kaisner steps forward.

"I'm sorry," he says to Nikolaas. "For whatever I said that triggered you. For not realizing how close to the edge you were. For—"

"No." Nikolaas cuts him off. "You did nothing wrong. I saw something tonight. Heard something. And I let it twist my perception." He takes a shaky breath. "I'm not well tonight. The curse is progressing, and I—" His voice breaks. "I might not be safe to be around anymore."

"Then we help you," Clarissa says fiercely. "We find a way to break the curse. Together. As family."

"I'm sorry too," Gavriil says, though he's looking at the floor. "Ivan was right, godsdamn him. I don't get to lecture anyone about control when I—" He stops. Looks at me. "When I did what I did."

"I was. But I shouldn't have brought it up tonight," Ivan admits. "Not at the party. Not when—"

"Yes, you should have," Dristan interrupts.

"Someone needed to say it. I just wish it hadn't been here."

"We all wish a lot of things," Juliette says quietly. "But wishing doesn't change what happened. Choosing to move forward does."

Luciana moves to Gavriil's side, taking his hand. "We're all broken," she says. "Every single one of us. But maybe that's what makes us family. The broken pieces choosing to stand together."

Anya shifts Katya, who's finally stopped crying. The toddler looks around at all of us with those wide, curious eyes, and then—impossibly—she giggles.

Makes more snow fall.

Claps her tiny hands like this is the best party she's ever seen.

And despite everything—despite the fighting and the tears and the near-disaster—we all start to laugh.

"She stopped us," Samara says, smiling through tears at the little wolf-witch. "Cooled everyone's tempers—*literally.*"

"She's practical that way," Vlad says proudly. "Takes after her mother."

"She's chaos," Anya corrects. "Takes after her father."

"Both can be true," I say.

I look around at all of them. My family. Standing in snow and ash, half their gifts unopened, the party in ruins around us. And I realize something.

This—right here, right now—this is what I wanted.

Not the perfect dinner. Not the flawless celebration. Not everyone getting along without conflict.

I wanted them to show up. To choose each other even when it's hard. To fight and break things and then stay to fix them.

That's family.

Not the highlight reel. Not the perfect moments we curate for the world to see.

But the messy truth underneath. The willingness to be broken together. To see each other's worst and still choose to stay.

16

CASSANDRA: WHAT REMAINS

The party doesn't continue. But it doesn't exactly end either.

Because apparently, when my family breaks something, they also fix it.

"I've got the tree," Gavriil announces, already moving toward the half-frozen, half-singed monstrosity. "Volodya, help me carry this disaster outside before it catches fire again or freezes the entire manor."

"On it." Vlad positions himself at the other end. Together, they hoist the ruined tree, ornaments falling and shattering as they navigate it toward the door.

His steel gaze cuts to mine. "Next year, perhaps skip the May Christmas?"

"Next year," I say firmly, "we're doing this again. And you're all coming."

Gavriil pauses at the doorway, the tree balanced precariously. "Cassandra—"

"You're coming," I repeat. "All of you."

He exchanges a look with Vlad, then nods. They maneuver the tree through the door with impressive shifter strength, as though it's weightless.

"I'll handle the snow," Samara says quietly. She's holding Nikolaas' hand, but there's determination in her maroon eyes. She closes them, and I feel her winter magic respond. The snow doesn't vanish—it gathers itself, swirling up into the air before flowing out the open windows like a white river.

Nikolaas watches her with something like awe. Like he's seeing her clearly for the first time tonight.

"Your magic has grown so much, Little Bear," he murmurs into her ear.

She blushes, her gaze drifting downwards.

It will only grow stronger from now on, I want to add. She's days away from reaching her twenty-first birthday—the age when a witch's power reaches its ultimate peak.

"The curtains are ruined," Luciana observes, already pulling down the singed fabric. "But the frames are intact. I can source replacements if—"

"I'll cover the costs," Nikolaas says. Everyone turns to look at him. "My fire. My damage. My responsibility."

"*Our* fire," Kaisner corrects quietly. He's on the other side of the room, helping Clarissa right an overturned chair. "*Our* damage. Let's split the bill."

The two dragons look at each other across the ruined parlor.

It's not forgiveness.

But it's acknowledgment. Responsibility. A first step.

"Well," Ivan drawls, appearing with a broom from gods know where. "If we're all playing house, someone should probably sweep up these ornaments before the baby starts crawling." He gestures at my belly. "Though knowing your child, they'll probably just make the glass grow back into ornaments through sheer magical force of will."

Despite everything, I laugh.

Juliette appears beside him with a dustpan. "Here. And try not to complain. You've never lifted a finger to clean anything in three centuries."

"Juliette," he gasps. "I'm a vampire with a bad rep—"

"You're helping." She presses the dustpan into his hands. "Bad reputation intact."

Dristan moves to my side, one arm around my waist. "You should sit down."

"I should help—"

"You've done enough." His voice is gentle but firm. "Let them take care of this. Let them take responsibility for what they've done."

I watch them work. Gavriil and Vlad returning from depositing the tree outside, immediately moving to help Luciana with the curtains. Samara directing the last of the snow out the windows while Nikolaas carefully picks up broken glass. Kaisner and Clarissa working together to straighten furniture. Ivan and Juliette bickering over the proper sweeping technique.

Anya trying to keep Katya from making more snow while simultaneously laughing at the chaos.

"This isn't how I pictured the evening ending," I admit.

"No?" Dristan's lips quirk. "You pictured something more catastrophic?"

"Less... collaborative destruction cleanup?"

Gavriil crosses to us, soot still streaking his face. "Cassandra. The way I spoke to Ivan, the way I let my temper—"

"Was very Ursa King of you," I interrupt. "Territorial. Protective. A little dramatic." I pause. "But you also threw yourself between two dragons to protect everyone in this room. So I think it balances out."

He looks like he wants to argue, but Luciana appears at his elbow. "We did what you asked," she says to me. "We came. We tried." She gives Gavriil a tender look. "That has to count for something."

"It does," I say softly. "It really does."

Nikolaas and Samara approach next. He still won't quite meet my eyes, but Samara squeezes my hand.

"Thank you," she whispers. "For inviting us. For trying to give us this. Even if it—"

"Exploded into dragon fire and magical snow?" I finish. "Yeah. But you're coming back next year anyway."

"Cassandra—"

"Next year," I repeat firmly. "Both of you. Because this is what family does. We show up. We make messes.

We clean them up together. And then we do it all over again."

Samara's eyes shine with unshed tears. "Next year," she agrees.

Kaisner and Clarissa are last. Clarissa hugs me fiercely. "What you did tonight mattered, Cassie," he says. "Even if right now it doesn't feel like it."

"My dining room is destroyed."

"Our family is learning," she corrects. "Learning that they can break things and still fix them. That they can fight and still choose each other." She pulls back, silver gleaming at the edges of her pale blue eyes. "That's worth a few burned curtains."

Kaisner extends his hand to me. "Thank you for having me. I know that put you in an impossible position."

"Everything about this family is impossible," I point out. "You fit right in."

He smiles—small, genuine. "Next May?"

"Absolutely."

One by one, they leave. Not fleeing the disaster, but departing like guests after any party. Tired but satisfied that they did what they could.

Finally, it's just me and Dristan and Vlad and Anya, standing in a parlor that's cleaner than it was but still clearly bears the scars of tonight's chaos.

"Well," Vlad says, surveying what remains. "That was—"

"Perfect," I say firmly.

They all stare at me.

"Cassandra," Dristan says carefully, "the tree is gone, the curtains are destroyed, there's still snow melting into the carpet, and two dragons nearly burned down your ancestral home."

"I know." I lean into him, one hand on my belly where the baby has finally settled. "But they all showed up. They tried. And when they broke things, they stayed to help fix them." I look around at the evidence of tonight's disaster. "That's family. Not the perfect moments. The messy ones where we choose each other anyway."

"She's losing it," Vlad stage-whispers to Anya.

"Pregnancy hormones," Anya whispers back.

"I can hear you both," I say. "And I'm not losing it. I'm choosing to see this as a success."

"A success." Dristan's tone is carefully neutral. "Your criteria for success have become quite flexible."

"My criteria for success," I correct, "have become realistic. Perfect Christmases are boring. Messy ones where everyone shows up despite the chaos? Where we fight and reconcile and clean up together? Those are real."

The baby stirs—gentle now, settled.

"See?" I say. "Even they agree."

Dristan kisses my temple. "Your optimism is terrifying."

"Your pessimism is challenging."

"And yet, you chose me." His voice is tender.

"Best choice I ever made," I whisper.

And looking around at the ruined parlor, at the

evidence of my family's spectacular disaster and their equally spectacular cleanup effort, I smile.

Because they came.

They fought and broke things and made enormous messes.

But they stayed.

They fixed what they could.

And they promised to come back next year.

That's what remains. Not perfection. Not the flawless Christmas I planned.

But something better.

Something real.

BEST CHRISTMAS EVER

The Seine is frozen.

Well, not entirely. Just the edges where the current slows near the stone embankments. But it's enough to catch my attention as I walk along the Quai Voltaire at three in the morning, collar turned up against the December wind that shouldn't exist in May.

Yes, December wind. In May.

Katya's snow didn't just cool tempers at the party—it followed us home. All of us. There are reports of unseasonable cold across Paris tonight, confused meteorologists babbling about unprecedented atmospheric conditions, and I know exactly what caused it.

A toddler wolf-witch having feelings.

Magic doesn't care about logic or seasons or scientific explanations. It cares about emotion. And tonight, that emotion was a desperate need for peace.

So now Paris is experiencing winter in spring, and

I'm walking alone beside a half-frozen river, trying to process what I witnessed at Deveraux Manor.

I told Juliette I needed air. Space to think. She understood—she always does. Kissed me and told me not to stay out until dawn, which is touching considering I've managed to avoid immolating myself for three centuries without supervision.

But she worries.

It's one of the things I love about her.

The city is empty at this hour. Just me and the river and the supernatural events of the evening pressing down like Katya's impossible snow.

You're still there, aren't you?

Yes, you. The one who's been following this story since I opened it with complaints about Christmas parties and pregnant witches and supernatural dysfunction masquerading as family.

I can feel you watching. Waiting to see if I learned anything. If the cynical vampire found meaning in the chaos.

Spoiler alert: I did.

But not the way you probably think.

A barge drifts past, its lights reflecting off the ice-crusted water. The captain—human, unaware of the supernatural drama that just rearranged his weather patterns—waves at me from the wheelhouse.

I wave back.

Three hundred years ago, I would have considered him prey. Food. A means to an end.

Now? He's just another person trying to navigate impossible waters.

Funny how perspective shifts.

At the party tonight, I picked a fight with Gavriil. Called him a hypocrite for lecturing dragons about control when he'd branded Cassandra. Pointed out that he hides behind words like "duty" and "necessity" while condemning others for their nature.

And he threw it back at me—hard.

Said I was a vampire who'd killed more people than I could count. That my kind murdered his father, so forgive him if he didn't trust my moral judgment.

Lumped me in with every vampire who'd ever existed because of what one of us did to his family.

Species prejudice wrapped in grief and called it justified.

And he wasn't entirely wrong.

Because I *am* a monster. I've killed more people than Gavriil has even met. I've lived three centuries on human blood, and while I'm discrete about it now—civilized, as we vampires like to pretend—the body count doesn't disappear because I've learned table manners.

Dristan made me what I am. Turned me without asking, without explaining what it would cost. I've spent three hundred years alternating between gratitude and resentment for that gift.

But tonight, watching Cassandra stand in that snow-covered parlor and talk about choice—about how we don't get to choose our nature but we do get to choose what we do with it—I realized something.

Dristan made me a vampire.

But I *chose* to become Ivan.

Every decision after that first bite—every person I spared, every kill I regretted, every relationship I built, every sarcastic comment I deployed to keep people at arm's length—that was me. Not the vampire nature. Not the blood hunger.

Me.

Making choices.

Just like Gavriil chose to brand Cassandra and then chose to apologize.

Just like Nikolaas is choosing to use that grimoire and will soon have to choose whether to let the curse consume him.

Just like Clarissa chose Kaisner despite her brother's fury, and Vlad chose to become an alpha despite being cast out by his birth pack, and Cassandra chose all of us despite every reason to walk away.

Choice.

It's the only thing that separates monsters from family.

And tonight, we chose family.

Badly. Imperfectly. With fighting and fire, and a toddler having to literally cool us down with magic snow.

But we chose it.

I reach the Pont Royal, where the streetlamps cast long shadows across the frozen river. Lovers have attached padlocks to railings further downstream—the Pont des Arts, mostly—symbolic imprisonment disguised as romance. Humans are strange creatures.

But then again, so are we.

A supernatural family held together by brands and curses and impossible bonds, locked to each other not by magic but by the stubborn refusal to give up.

Maybe we're not so different from those padlocks after all.

My phone vibrates. A text from Juliette:

> The bed is cold without you. Come home.

Home.

When did 1 Rue Saint Thomas d'Aquin become home? When did Juliette stop being the ghost I mourned for three centuries and become the woman sharing my present instead of haunting my past?

When did this become real?

I think it was tonight. Watching her stand with her family—because they are her family now, just as they're mine—and defend them even when they were being absolutely insufferable.

Watching her take responsibility for enabling Gavriil's brand because she was the Head Witch who gave consent.

Watching her refuse to let him shoulder all the blame alone.

That's when it became real.

Not perfect. Not easy.

But real.

I turn away from the river, from the frozen edges and the drifting barges. My apartment is only a few minutes' walk from here—back along the quai, turn onto Rue Saint Thomas d'Aquin.

Toward Juliette.

Toward home.

But before I go—before I leave you here on the banks of the Seine with nothing but Katya's magical snow and the echoes of choices made—let me tell you what I learned tonight.

At the beginning of this story, I told you Christmas was a human holiday. That vampires don't celebrate the birth of a god who would condemn us. That the whole affair was performative nonsense designed to make people feel better about their mortality.

I was wrong.

Not about the god part—I still have theological objections that three centuries haven't resolved.

But about Christmas itself.

Cassandra set that tree on fire three times tonight. Three times. And each time, she just waved away the smoke, laughed, and kept decorating. Because timing didn't matter. Perfection didn't matter. What mattered was that we were all there.

She didn't throw a Christmas party because she believed in miracles.

She threw it because she believed in *us*.

In our ability to show up despite our damage. To choose each other despite our sins. To keep trying even when it would be so much easier—so much more sensible—to walk away.

And we did.

We showed up.

We tried.

We failed spectacularly and then tried again.

That's better than a Christmas miracle.

That's family.

Not the kind you're born into. Not the kind that's easy or comfortable or free from conflict.

The kind you build. One disastrous party at a time. One choice to stay instead of leaving. One decision to forgive without forgetting, to apologize without erasing, to keep showing up even when showing up means watching dragons nearly kill each other over prophecies that may or may not come true.

My phone vibrates again.

I laugh out loud, the sound echoing off the empty street.

Three hundred years, and she still makes me laugh.

So here's my final thought for you, dear darkling:

Was tonight the best Christmas in centuries?

By any objective measure, no.

It was a disaster. A beautiful, chaotic, absolutely ridiculous disaster.

But it was ours.

That's the real story.

Not that we're perfect. Not that we're healed. Not that we've overcome our trauma or erased our sins or become better people.

But that we're trying.

And trying—stubborn, imperfect, absolutely chaotic trying—is the only miracle that matters.

Joyeux Noël, darkling.

May you have the courage to choose your own impossible family.

Even when—especially when—it would be easier to walk alone.

With all the holiday cheer I'm able to muster,
Ivan Lockhart.

ABOUT THE AUTHOR

 Silvana G. Sánchez is the USA TODAY bestselling author of sinfully addictive dark fantasy new adult novels *Ash and Snow, Steel and Stone, Written in Blood,* and more paranormal and fantasy romance stories, including the *Vesely Academy* series. She lives in Mexico with her husband, son, and two adorable Shih-Tzus she calls her dragons. When not plotting away in her writing den, she's known to poke eyes in her practice as an ophthalmologist.

For more information:
silvanagsanchez.com
sgs.author@gmail.com

9 781971 239002